"Just what do you expect me to do, *señor*?"

Jan fought to control her emotions. "Doesn't it concern you that you have just taken away my livelihood?"

"It concerns me, Miss Shelley, and I have a position you can fill." Carlos grasped her arms and pulled her slowly to him. "A position you will fill very well." He glared at her with dark, fathomless eyes, and Jan shuddered. "The position, Miss Shelley, is that of my mistress."

Jan pushed away from him abruptly. "I find your offer outrageous," she said firmly, "and the answer is no."

"It isn't an offer," he said, his manner deceptively mild. "It is an order."

Liza Goodman is a new author with a powerful, evocative writing style. Her stories capture readers' imaginations, inviting them to embark on a romantic fantasy.

Eagle's Revenge

Liza Goodman

Harlequin Books

TORONTO • NEW YORK • LONDON
AMSTERDAM • PARIS • SYDNEY • HAMBURG
STOCKHOLM • ATHENS • TOKYO • MILAN

Original hardcover edition published in 1987
by Mills & Boon Limited

ISBN 0-373-17028-9

Harlequin Romance first edition December 1988

To my husband,
without whose help and support
I should find it very difficult
to write at all,
and to Roma who has encouraged
me to keep writing and
who has earned the right to say
'I told you so.'

CHAPTER ONE

THE crowded lift stopped at last on the ground floor. Jan heaved a sigh of relief and edged her way to the door. It hadn't been a very good idea to come shopping in Birmingham in a heatwave on her day off from work. She resigned herself to waiting until everyone else had forced their way through the doors, feeling she would suffocate if she didn't get into the open air soon. At last her way was clear and she was able to step from the lift.

She ran down the stairs, across the entrance hall and out of the building, kicking against something heavy as she gained the underpass. She looked down at the obstacle she had stumbled over and, picking it up, stared at the fine leather wallet, automatically opening it to search for the owner's name and address. She drew a breath of amazement. She had never seen so much money; there must have been hundreds of pounds. She turned back towards the store: she must turn the wallet over to one of the staff before someone thought she was stealing it. She was brought up short by a hard hand tightening round her arm with a grip that hurt.

'That is my wallet, you little thief.' His voice was very deep and Jan looked up to see a man looming over her. He's a giant, she thought, as her eyes travelled over what seemed to be acres of cream lightweight jacket and pale tan shirt. His tie combined the two shades, she noticed, before her gaze met eyes that looked at her with a contempt she had never received before. They were black, under well-shaped brows drawn together in anger. His nose was strong, as was his jaw, and his mouth was grimly set in a straight line that couldn't entirely disguise its sensuality. His hair was thick and as black as his eyes.

Jan gulped as she took in how powerful he was, his broad shoulders denoting muscles like iron. Six feet three inches at least. She pulled away from him, trying to break free from his grip. He merely tightened his fingers round her arm and Jan cried out in pain.

'You're hurting me. Let me go. What right have you to hold me prisoner?'

He smiled and a shiver ran down her spine. It was a smile that had been born in icy wastes and promised many things, all of them unpleasant.

'The right of every citizen to stop a thief.'

'I'm not a thief,' Jan said indignantly.

'This belongs to you, then?' He took the wallet from her limp fingers and put it in his pocket.

'No, I found it. I was going to give it to one of the staff. You say it is yours, but how do I know that? You could have seen me pick it up.'

'I did, but before I could say anything you were counting the money.' His mouth tightened. 'I will save you the trouble. There are five hundred pounds in that wallet; think of that, my little thief, and grieve to know you won't touch a penny of it.'

'That still doesn't make you the owner.'

'You don't have to take my word. Come with me.' He started towards the store but Jan dug her heels in.

'Wait a minute, I'm not going anywhere with you.'

'You are coming to the security office and there we can determine the owner of the wallet. I shall ask the store detective to send for the police and they can search you. It's certain you've got other trifles you have picked up.'

'I haven't!' Jan gasped, feeling she had walked into a nightmare. 'I picked the wallet up but I was going to hand it in. Oh, why won't you believe me?'

'I don't trust any woman to tell the truth,' he sneered, 'especially when she's caught red-handed. Now, are you coming on your own two feet or do I carry you?'

Jan looked at him in dismay; he meant every word. She was about to admit defeat and agree to accompany him when shouts and laughter exploded round them and a group of young people dressed in colourful garments, their hair all colours of the rainbow, surged across their path.

For a moment Jan was dazed by the sheer noise, then, taking advantage of the crush of bodies, she twisted free and ran as fast as she could in the direction of Corporation Street. She heard a deep-voiced command for her to stop, then it was swallowed by the traffic as she raced down the busy street. Her frantic pace slowed as she neared the station and she became aware that people were turning to look at her. She glanced over her shoulder as she walked quickly into the station but the tall man was nowhere in sight.

Jan drew a breath of relief; he obviously hadn't thought it worth his while to follow her. He had his wallet back and that was all he wanted. Even as the thought came into her head she knew it wasn't completely true. She had a strong suspicion that no one took anything from him without paying heavily. How she knew that after only such a short contact with him she didn't know, but with a conviction that had nothing to do with reason she was certain that if he ever saw her again he would—— She sank down on the seat of an empty carriage. She didn't know what he would do, she only knew he had frightened her more than anything or anyone ever had before.

She leaped to her feet and looked out of the window. Oh, why didn't the train start? She cast anxious glances along the platform but there was no one resembling him in sight. The train started with a jerk and she resumed her seat, relief washing over her as they cleared the station and the tall man was left behind. She took out her comb and handbag mirror and it wasn't until her pale blonde hair was tidy that she started to shake.

She dropped the comb and buried her face in her hands. During the race to the station and the tense minutes before the train left she had managed to hold her thoughts at bay; now they hit her with force. Shame and disgust overwhelmed her so strongly she felt ill. Shame that anyone even a stranger, should think she was a thief, and disgust at the way she had reacted. Running away would only have convinced him she was guilty. She wiped her eyes with a tissue. It didn't matter what he thought; she knew she was innocent. Not for a moment had she contemplated keeping the wallet, even though he wouldn't miss the money it contained, if his appearance was anything to go by.

She groaned as she recalled the contempt in his eyes. She had never felt so humiliated in her life and it was all a mistake. Once more Jan regretted her hasty flight. She should have stayed; he would be a hard man to convince of anything once he had made up his mind but he would listen to a reasonable explanation, she was sure. Jan shook her head. How did she know that? He wasn't even English; his accent was slight, nearly perfect, but apart from that his clothing was that of a warmer climate, Italy perhaps.

For the rest of the journey she determinedly read a paperback she had brought with her, shutting her mind firmly against the stranger, and it wasn't until she picked up her bag on arrival at Derby that she realised she had lost the carrier bag containing the three jumpers she had bought in John Lewis. She choked back a laugh that threatened to turn into a sob. The day had been a complete disaster.

During the next few days Jan struggled to rid herself of the image of a strong, unforgettable face. He invaded her dreams, travelled home and stayed with her until she went to bed, and came between her and her work, even when she was seated at her desk as she was now. She couldn't forget the way he had looked at her as if she was utterly beneath his notice. Jan clenched her fists at her sides; if she ever met him again she would tell him just what she thought of a man who condemned without any real evidence.

She looked down at the drawing on her desk. Until now she had been more than satisfied with her life. Her work as a designer in the Eagle Potteries near Derby was rewarding and fulfilling. It was a young company, part of a bigger one in Spain, and she counted herself fortunate to be part of a new and thriving enterprise.

Jan sighed, pushed her hair away from her face and concentrated on the harebell she was painting. She really must put the incident in Birmingham out of her mind. She acknowledged wryly that the man had made far too strong an impression on her and that she wished she had met him under different circumstances. She bit her lip as she smeared the leaf she was painting. How could she dwell so much on a man she didn't know when there was Wade?

Wade ... She still couldn't believe anyone so

marvellous could love someone as ordinary as she was. Jan stroked the third finger of her left hand, a dreamy smile on her lips. They were getting engaged the next time he came home. Wade was the head of the sales team and at present he was at the parent pottery in Spain and would be for several weeks to come.

She had hoped Wade would give her a ring before he went to Spain, but he wanted to give her one worthy of her beauty, he had said, laughing and kissing her until she collapsed breathless into his arms. He was so happy, Jan hadn't liked to tell him that the cheapest ring would be as splendid as the expensive one he was determined she should have.

She thought longingly of him, conjuring up his fair, smiling image, but a dark, frowning face came between her and Wade's. She picked up her brush with an angry jerk that sent spots of pale pink shooting across her desk. She muttered under her breath as she hastily wiped the paint up. What was wrong with her, that even when she was thinking of Wade the dark stranger should intrude?

The door of her office opened and she looked up from the delicate painting, starting to her feet as she saw the tall fair-haired man smiling at her.

'Wade,' she cried, her violet eyes filling with pleasure. 'I didn't expect you back for weeks!'

'I couldn't stay away any longer.' He kissed her until she murmured in response and he lifted his head and laughed softly.

'I've missed you so much, Jan. It's seemed like twelve months, not twelve weeks.'

'I find that hard to believe,' she returned, her lips lifting at the corners. 'What about all those Spanish lovelies?'

'As you say, all very lovely but not as beautiful as you

are. Have I told you lately that I love you?' He swung
her off her feet and kissed her hard before setting her
down again.

'My uncle died two weeks ago,' he went on. 'I
couldn't get here in time to attend the funeral but it
appears I'm his heir and I have to settle his estate.' He
threw his hands above his head. 'I've been at the lawyers
all morning and I'm due back as soon as I have reported
to the boss, but I couldn't leave without seeing you.' He
kissed her again, his good humour back in full force. He
looked at his watch.

'I shall have to go, Jan. Old Hartley will have a fit if he
finds out I'm in the building before I get to him.' He
pulled her to him and kissed her lightly. 'I'll pick you up
at eight and we'll have dinner. My uncle left me quite a
bit of money and we must talk and make plans. Until
then, Jan.' He kissed her once more and left to make his
report. Jan sat down, her eyes glowing, and hugged
herself in excitement. Wade said they would make plans;
perhaps those plans would include a wedding.

The second-hand Mini was a new acquisition and Jan
drove carefully to the cottage she rented in a village three
miles from the pottery. She had been lucky, she mused,
as she looked round the long, low living-room furnished
in green and brown that, together with a small kitchen,
composed the ground floor. A bedroom decorated in
white and yellow with a matching bathroom occupied
the first floor and she was more than happy with her
home.

Jan thought lovingly of her Aunt Mary who had
brought her up after her parents had been killed in a
plane crash. She had died when Jan was eighteen,
leaving Jan enough money to attend art college, and six

years later she was well on the way to achieving
everything she dreamed of. And above all there was
Wade. She smiled as she slipped into a silky cream dress
that was only a shade or two lighter than the hair she
piled on top of her head and secured with an ebony comb
she had found in an antique shop in Derby.

The comb made her think of Spain, and a small
wrinkle appeared between her eyes. Would Wade have
to go back? She hoped he wouldn't. She pouted her lips
at her reflection and wished her skin wasn't so white.
True, she had delicate colour on her high cheekbones,
but against a Spanish beauty she would look washed out.
Wade had a marvellous tan; he hadn't got that in an
office. For a moment another, darker face flashed in
front of her eyes before she resolutely continued her
inspection of her mirrored image.

Her figure wasn't bad; her breasts were a bit too full
but her waist and hips were slim enough and her legs
long and slender. Her five feet three inches to Wade's six
feet was just right; she dismissed the stranger who could
give Wade several inches and tugged at her belt angrily.
Couldn't she keep him out of her mind even when she
was dressing to go out with Wade? The doorbell chimed
and she snatched up a lacy shawl before opening the
door.

Wade kissed her and, putting his hand under her
elbow, handed her into his car. It was a new one, a sleek
grey Jaguar. She raised her eyebrows and he grinned.

'How do you like her, Jan? I only took delivery today.'

'That was quick work,' she said. 'You've only just got
back.'

'Can't waste time when you know what you want, and
it's not the only dream that will come true, thanks to the
old man.'

Jan frowned. Wade's glee in acquiring the car was understandable—she knew he had had to fight to get where he was and for everything he had—but so soon after his uncle's death it struck a false note.

'I've booked a table here, Jan. I think you'll like it,' he said with satisfaction as he brought the car smoothly to a halt before a small inn several miles from her cottage. Jan looked at the unpretentious building with surprise. Wade had written a lot about the places he had visited in Spain and large fashionable restaurants had seemed much in favour. She frowned; it almost seemed as if he didn't want to be seen with her. She looked at his smiling face and her worry disappeared.

'It's lovely, Wade,' she said as they settled in the small dining-room, and certainly the food was very good. Wade ordered white wine for Jan and beer for himself and a happy glow spread over her. She smiled at him, the subdued lighting making her deep violet eyes look mysterious and her hair shine softly, small tendrils floating round her face like silver floss.

The evening was proving to be all she had hoped. Wade talked amusingly of his time in Spain while leaving her in no doubt of his delight in being home.

'You're looking very lovely tonight, Jan. Have I ever told you I prefer blondes?' he said. She laughed, feeling happier than she had done since her visit to Birmingham. Now why did she have to think of that at this moment?

She turned her head, compelled by an invisible tug at her nerves, to meet dark eyes looking intently at her. She caught her breath and turned back to Wade. The man she had met in Birmingham was sitting at the next table with such a look of arrogant disgust at finding himself in the same room that a shudder she couldn't control ran through her.

'Are you all right, Jan? You're very pale. You haven't had too much wine?' Jan forced herself to smile, though she felt more like screaming. To discover she hadn't left behind her the man who haunted her dreams was a shock she could have done without. Whatever was he doing here?

'I'm fine, Wade. You were going to tell me about your plans.' Jan leaned towards him, willing herself not to respond to the urge to turn round again.

'There's such a lot I want to do, Jan, but it will have to wait until I get back from Spain. Yes,' at Jan's dismayed exclamation, 'I have to go back, and would you believe tomorrow? It shouldn't be too long, though.' He put his knife and fork down and looked at Jan, a half smile on his face.

'I don't intend to go mad or throw my job up. Most of Uncle's money is wisely invested and will bring in a good extra income.'

Jan drank the last of her wine, wishing Wade would finish his drink so that they could leave; she still felt dark eyes boring into her. She moved her shoulders uneasily. Her back felt warmer than the rest of her and though she told herself it was sheer imagination she was acutely uncomfortable and was having difficulty in stopping herself trembling. She didn't know why he had such an effect on her ... Yes, she did. She was downright angry that anyone, even a stranger, should think she would steal anything.

Wade leaned over the table and kissed her on her lips. She blushed and drew back, only too conscious of the waves of anger and disapproval coming from the next table.

'Wade,' she protested. He smiled, his blue eyes looking at her with a warmth that made the colour rush back into her face.

'Not the place or the time,' he said ruefully, 'but you look so lovely I couldn't resist it.' He took her hand in his. 'I've seen just the ring for you, Jan, but I didn't have time to get it. It's first on my list as soon as I get back to Spain.' He kissed her hand and Jan would have been thrilled, but she could feel the contempt and aversion of the dark man as if they were tangible things, and she was thankful when Wade suggested they should leave.

CHAPTER TWO

'HAVE you heard?' Gina Trent said breathlessly as she put Jan's mug of coffee down with such force that the liquid spilled on to the desk. 'Oh, sorry,' Gina said, dabbing at the desk with her hankie. 'It's so exciting, isn't it?'

'What is?' asked Jan, moving her papers out of the way and mopping up with a handful of tissues. 'I wish you'd be more careful, Gina, you could have ruined my entire morning's work.'

'Sorry,' Gina said again. 'You haven't heard, have you, Jan?'

'Obviously not, and just as obviously you are dying to tell me.' Gina's blue eyes danced with excitement.

'You must be the last person to know,' she said gleefully.

'Don't keep me in suspense,' Jan said, laughing in spite of herself.

'The boss has arrived.' Gina's dark curls seemed to take on a life of their own as she practically danced round the room.

'I didn't know Mr Hartley had been away.'

'No, no,' Gina said impatiently. 'Not Mr H. The boss from Spain, Carlos del Raimondes, and he's as gorgeous as his name. Just wait till you see him; he's got every girl in the place wild.'

'I wonder why he's come?' Jan said thoughtfully, an unexplained chill touching her spine.

'Don't know and don't care. I only hope he stays a

16

long time; brighten the place up no end, he will. He's a millionaire several times over and his grandfather's heir as well.' She shook her head mournfully. 'I quite fancy marrying a very rich man—don't you?—but he wouldn't look at me.' She whisked Jan's half-empty mug away before she could protest and shot through the door.

The next few days slid past slowly. The whole office, the female part anyway, was plunged into gloom by the departure of Carlos del Raimondes after a stay of only two days, but Jan could only wait hopefully for a letter from Wade and she was thankful when the weekend arrived. She roamed the countryside for hours before deciding to work on an idea she had for a series of plates and spent the rest of the weekend at her desk. There was a brief note from Wade saying he was very busy and would write more fully later, but a further two weeks went by without word from him.

At last, to Jan's delight, Wade telephoned on Monday morning, just as she was getting ready for work. She lifted the receiver and answered impatiently.

'Hello, Jan. Aren't you pleased to hear from me?'

'Wade! But you're in Spain,' she said foolishly, all her fears falling away at the sound of his voice.

'I am, love,' he said teasingly. 'We do have telephones here, you know.' His voice sharpened. 'You sound surprised to hear from me.'

'I am.'

'You shouldn't be. I said I would phone you at this time in my last letter. You did get it?'

'No, Wade, I haven't heard from you since you returned to Spain.' She held the phone away as Wade shouted with rage.

'Oh, love,' he said after a moment. 'I'm so sorry. I've written you four letters and I've had one from you.'

'Then you have another two to come,' Jan said,

feeling a heavy weight roll from her shoulders. 'I'm so glad you phoned, Wade.'

'So am I. My poor love, what must you have been thinking?'

They chatted for a few minutes then Wade said he must go.

'It won't be long now, love. Another three weeks and I should be home, so don't worry if my letters don't get through.'

'I won't,' Jan said happily.

'I'll phone you again. Oh, there is something you can do for me. I was going to phone someone whom I've known for years and who's just started work at the office but I haven't time now. Will you pass a message on for me? Say I'll phone one evening. Must go now, love.'

'Wait, you haven't told me the name or the office number.'

'Oh, lord, so I haven't. It's Phillip Johnson, room three, fourth floor. Don't forget, love, I wouldn't like him to think I don't keep my promises.'

'I won't. I'll go as soon as I get in.' Jan put down the receiver and whirled round the room; she felt as light as thistledown when only a few minutes before she had had a fellow feeling for Atlas.

She finished dressing in a lightweight suit of almond brown with a blouse of a darker shade. Cream sandals completed an outfit in which she felt happy. She parked her Mini next to an opulent Rolls-Royce and, wondering vaguely whose it was, took the lift to the fourth floor as soon as she had deposited her coat and handbag in her office. She would get Wade's errand over before she started work.

The long corridor, closely covered in thick blue carpet, was so quiet she felt like an intruder. She told herself not to be silly and walked along until she came to room three. There was no name, only the number, and Jan hesitated before knocking and opening the door. The office was large and richly furnished and quite empty. Jan wondered if she should leave a message but the magnificent desk was completely bare.

Jan grimaced. She had left her pen in her bag, so she would have to come back, or, better still, use the internal phone. She closed the door thankfully behind her. The lavish furnishings were having a depressing effect and she wanted to return to the happy mood left by Wade's phone call.

Once back in her own office she spread her new designs on the desk. The first one was finished, waiting only for the bone china plate that would complete the glowing colours. A blue and gold butterfly danced in mid-air above a clump of dandelions, the deep gold of the flowers toning with the butterfly's wings while the airiness of the dandelion clocks completed an unusual and saleable plate. If Mr Hartley approved she planned to do five more with different butterflies and flowers.

The morning went well and Jan sighed with satisfaction as she put her new design on Mr Hartley's desk as she went to lunch. It was too lovely a day to spend her precious free time in a crowded restaurant so, buying sandwiches, she sat in a nearby park and ate her meal watching the birds. The time passed all too quickly and she was soon back at her desk.

She had just started work when Gina burst in.

'He's back, Jan,' she said before Jan could speak.

'Who is?' Jan asked, refusing to be impressed.

'The boss, that's who, and he wants to see you. Señor del Raimondes. Hurry, Jan, he's rung down twice already and the last time he wanted to know how long you took for lunch. I don't think he likes being kept waiting.'

Jan checked her make-up in the small mirror hanging by the window. Her suit was just right and she was pleased she had coiled her long fair hair in a french pleat that morning. She looked competent and cool, even if she didn't feel it.

She took the executive lift to the top floor, wondering why Carlos del Raimondes wanted to see a lowly artist. Perhaps Mr Hartley had shown him the butterfly plate and he wanted to discuss it. Yes, unlikely as it seemed, that must be it. That settled to her satisfaction, Jan smiled at the girl in the outer office, who waved her towards the inner office.

'Go in, Jan.' She put her hands together and raised her eyes to the ceiling. 'I hope you can cool his temper,' she added in a low voice as Jan tapped on the door. A deep voice told her to come in and she obeyed, smoothing her hair nervously as she turned the handle. Something about the voice with its slight accent was disturbingly familiar. She closed the door quietly behind her and turned to face the man seated behind the desk.

Shock and recognition flashed in Jan's violet eyes, matched by the expression in the black ones glaring back at her. He rose and came round the desk with the speed of a hungry tiger. No, not a tiger; he was like the eagle his potteries were named after, and just as swift and dangerous.

'Oh, no,' Jan moaned, realising with horror that Carlos del Raimondes, the owner of the potteries here and in Spain and goodness knew what else besides, was the same man who had accused her of stealing his wallet.

'What the devil are you doing here?' he roared.

'You sent for me,' Jan managed to say, gathering her scattered wits with difficulty.

'You are Jacinta Shelley?' He sounded amazed and

Jan had time to think he was the most striking man she had ever seen, as well as one of the most powerful. He towered above her and she wished she could run. Instead she lifted her head and stared straight at him, inwardly quailing before the rage in his eyes.

'I might have known. Once a thief, always a thief.'

'I am not a thief, *señor*. I told you the truth about your wallet.'

'Did you?' he sneered. 'You must forgive me if I believe the evidence of my own eyes. My wallet isn't important, but the reason why you were on the fourth floor this morning is. You have no business there, Miss Shelley so perhaps you will tell me why you were seen coming out of room three and how you got into an office that is always kept locked?'

Jan stared at him, his words going round and round in her mind and making no sense.

'Well, Miss Shelley, I am waiting and it will do you no good to make up one of your fairytales as you did about my wallet.'

Jan's colour rose angrily. He still believed she had intended to steal his money, but the rest of his words were complete nonsense to her. 'Room three wasn't locked and I assure you I had a reason for being there.'

He leaned against the desk, a gleam in his narrowed eyes. 'Then let me into the secret,' he said quietly.

Jan stiffened; his quiet tone threatened more than if he had shouted. 'I was asked to give a message to someone in room three. I knocked then tried the door. It opened quite easily; I didn't have to use a jemmy.'

'Not even a key?' The question hung in the air with a menace that was almost tangible.

'Why should I need a key to deliver a simple message?

I was going to try again later.'

'I am sure you would have if it had been necessary but it wasn't, was it? You achieved your objective the first time.' He straightened and took a step nearer to her, bringing him so close she could see the silky texture of the luxuriant lashes that prevented her seeing the expression in his eyes. His eyelids lifted and Jan stepped back at the fury she saw directed at her.

His hand shot out and grasped her wrist.

'You are not leaving this office until I get a satisfactory answer. You are an expert at running away but this time it won't work.'

'I have no intention of running,' Jan said, glaring at him.

'No? I think differently.' He gestured at the chair placed near the desk.

'Sit down, Miss Shelley, and prepare to tell the truth for once in your life.'

Jan stiffened with indignation. He was the most hateful man she had ever met. What right had he to call her a liar?

'I always tell the truth,' she said, evoking a vision of Aunt Mary, a smile on her face as she had told Jan it was the only way to go on. Aunt Mary had a fund of sayings and they all related to the right way to 'go on'. She was brought out of her momentary lapse into the past by the sarcastic voice of the man who still held her wrist in a painful grip.

'You have a smug little smile on those seductive lips of yours,' he said in a voice that reminded her of thick cream filled with ground glass. 'Have you thought of a good reason for being inside room three?'

'How did you know I went into the office?' Jan said,

regretting the question as she saw the black eyes harden into jet.

'So you admit it? You were seen, so a denial won't do you any good.'

'I have no wish to deny anything, Señor del Raimondes. I have already given you my reason for visiting room three. I went into the office thinking I could leave a message for Mr Johnson but there wasn't a pad or pen available and as I had neither with me I left immediately. I didn't steal anything, if that is what you are saying.'

'That is exactly what I am saying, Miss Shelley. You not only had a key to the office, but one to the desk, from which you removed a highly secret document. The game is played out, Miss Shelley; your dreams of living in the sun on the proceeds from your theft are over. The only sunshine you will see for several years will be through prison bars.' Jan's hand went to her head as the room swung round and round. She swayed and he released her hand and pushed her into the chair.

'Sit down. I don't want to touch you again as I shall be obliged to do if you faint.' Jan leaned against the padded back of the chair, her eyes closed while she fought for control. She wouldn't allow her tormentor the satisfaction of knowing the despair she felt of ever making him believe her. Neither would she cry in front of him. She straightened her spine, tilting her head until she met his eyes, and stared defiantly into black depths that threatened unnamed horrors. She took a deep breath and clasped her trembling hands in her lap.

'I don't understand any of this,' she said as calmly as she could. 'You obviously think I've done something against you but that's not true. I was asked to take a simple message to Phillip Johnson, the door of the office wasn't locked and I didn't touch the desk.'

He stood very still with an expression that changed slowly into incredulity.

'I have met many opportunists, Miss Shelley, including thieves and liars, but never one like you. It will do you no good to keep repeating your feeble story. There is no Phillip Johnson on the fourth floor.'

'There must be. Wade . . .' She broke off as he came to life and hauled her out of the chair.

'What did you say your accomplice's name was?' he demanded.

'I haven't got an accomplice but if I had I wouldn't tell you anything.' Her words ended on a strangled scream as his mouth descended on hers in a punishing kiss that ground her soft lips painfully against her teeth. She struggled furiously but he pulled her close to him, her arms trapped between them, and slowly a warmth spread through her and her doubled fists relaxed against his silk shirt through which she could feel the powerful muscles of his chest. His kiss changed and his lips caressed hers until they opened of their own accord. He uttered an exclamation deep in his throat and his tongue invaded and explored the inner softness of her mouth. Jan came to her senses abruptly. She pulled away, taking him by surprise, and he let her go, staring at her with an awareness that ran through her like an electric shock.

Breathing raggedly, as if she had just taken part in a marathon, Jan sat down. She didn't think her legs would support her any longer and to collapse at his feet would be the final humiliation. She brushed a wisp of hair from her hot face and stole a look at the man who was once more leaning against the desk as if nothing had happened. His lips lifted in a grim smile as he surveyed her rumpled appearance.

'I must apologise,' he said smoothly. 'It is not my usual practice to kiss traitors, however beautiful.' He shook his head as if puzzled by his own actions.

'I am not a traitor,' Jan said, fiercely rejecting the pleasure of being called beautiful, 'and I can only say once more that I haven't taken anything from room three.'

'Then I am waiting to hear your reason, your good reason,' he drawled, emphasising the 'good' sarcastically, 'for being on the fourth floor.'

Jan, mentally apologising to Wade for bringing his name into such a disastrous interview, told him just why she had ventured to the fourth floor.

'I didn't know it was out of bounds,' she finished with a sarcasm matching his. 'Neither did Mr Felton or he wouldn't have asked me to go there.'

'Are you sure he did? Phillip Johnson's office is on the fifth floor. It is number three, but he has been there since the pottery started.' He paused, leaning towards her, his eyes boring into hers.

'It was your lucky day when Wade Felton asked you to take a message to Phillip Johnson. It handed you the opportunity you wanted. It was a pity your luck let you down and you were seen leaving the office, and doubly unfortunate that I sent for the formula not ten minutes later. It has taken time to gather the facts together and I still have to contact Felton in Spain but there is no doubt in my mind that you are guilty of stealing something that has taken me three years to perfect.'

He pulled her from her chair and shook her, his fingers biting into her arms.

'Where is it? I know it isn't in your office because I searched it myself when you were out. Who did you pass

it to?' Jan's eyes filled with tears and she could only
shake her head dumbly, afraid that if she attempted to
speak she would break down and beg him to believe her.
She didn't know why it was so important he should
think she was innocent, she only knew she couldn't bear
him to look at her as if he loathed her.

'Well, Miss Shelley, there is no way you are getting
out of here until you tell me what you have done with my
formula.' The caustic tone enabled Jan to achieve a
measure of control. She shook back her hair that had
partly fallen from its neat pleat and was tumbling round
her shoulders, fully aware that he followed every
movement.

'I have never set eyes on your precious formula. I
don't know what it is and I don't want to know.'

'Oh, I think you do know,' he said softly and Jan
shivered, a trickle of fear tracing its way down her
spine. 'You knew just what you were after,' he went on.
'Who did you sell it to, Miss Shelley? There are several
of our competitors who would pay well for my new
glaze.'

Jan ran the tip of her tongue over lips that were
suddenly dry, not noticing that his eyes followed the
gesture. The new glaze; no wonder he was livid. She had
heard rumours about the miracle glaze Carlos del
Raimondes had invented and she had looked forward to
seeing its effects on her own work in due course.

'Please believe me, I know nothing about your
formula and I am very sorry it is missing,' she said
sincerely.

'Then you will be pleased to learn that the glaze is
safe, the formula you sold was one that hadn't worked
out. Your customer won't be pleased with you, Miss
Shelley, when he tries to make it work, I am glad to say.'

A wave of relief washed over Jan and she smiled at him, making him catch his breath at the way it lit up and deepened the colour of her eyes and brought an added beauty to her delicate features.

'The fact that you stole a worthless piece of paper doesn't absolve you, Miss Shelley. You are still as guilty as hell. Tell me,' he enquired softly, 'if you had been successful in stealing my wallet, would that have satisfied you or would you still have gone ahead with your plan this morning? Is your greed for money so great you would rsk anything to gain it?'

'Nothing I can say will convince you I am innocent?' Jan asked after a silence that seemed to stretch to eternity.

'Nothing,' he answered.

Jan wondered when she would wake up from the nightmare she was having. She glanced out of the large window and saw a jet winging its way across the sky and for a moment she wished she was one of the passengers.

'You have no proof that I stole your formula.'

'I have an eye-witness,' he answered grimly.

'Who only saw me come out of the office, and as I have already admitted being there you will need more than that.' She got up and took a tentative step towards the door.

'If you have finished, *señor*, I will get back to work.'

'Not here, Miss Shelley. You are suspended from this moment.'

'You can't do that. I shall report you to the industrial tribunal. Whatever you might be able to do in Spain doesn't apply here.'

'I think it does when it concerns theft, and you are only suspended until I decide what to do with you.'

Jan drew a breath, but one look at the hard mouth and cold eyes stifled the words unborn.

'You and your kind, Miss Shelley are parasites, only too ready to take advantage of other people.' He opened a drawer in his desk and held out a print. Jan took it and cried out at the beauty that glowed up at her from the pictured vase.

'It's beautiful! Is this the new glaze? I don't wonder you are livid at the attempt to steal it!'

A brown hand came between Jan and the print, and long fingers replaced it in the drawer.

'Almost I believe you, but not quite; you were the only unauthorised person on the fourth floor this morning. I don't accuse you of stealing the first formula from Spain, that was your accomplice, obviously, and just as obviously it will save time if you identify him.'

'I know nothing about any of this. I can't make you believe me but that doesn't make me guilty. May I ask what you are going to do?' Jan said quietly.

He stared at her in silence until Jan was at screaming point. She raised her head and met a look she couldn't understand. He put one hand on the desk, leaning slightly against it, and looked her over from head to feet. He took his time and Jan blushed as his gaze travelled over her shapely legs, her hips and small waist to her breasts, where he lingered for what seemed a long time. He examined her face feature by feature, dwelling on her mouth, then he smiled and Jan wished he hadn't. It was a cruel twist of his lips that made her shake with fear.

'You are to leave here at once; you are not to enter your office again. I will be in touch with you in a few days.' He turned away, dismissing her from both his office and his mind, and after a few stunned moments Jan left quietly.

She didn't remember leaving the building or driving her car back home and it wasn't until the light faded from the sky that she realised she must have been sitting in her cottage window for hours.

CHAPTER THREE

THE next three days were dreadful. Jan washed, dressed, ate and went to bed at regular intervals like an automaton. Time, her time, was suspended until she heard from Carlos del Raimondes. By the morning of the fourth day she was beginning to feel again. All this time she had existed in a deep freeze and now the ice was melting. She tried to stop it but inevitably she came out of her trance and anguished thoughts of Wade crowded into her mind.

What would he think when he heard, as of course he soon would? Jan laughed unhappily, the sound shattering the silent void she had lived in since she had been suspended. The office grapevine was very efficient and by now Wade would have heard more than one version of the theft. He wouldn't believe she had anything to do with it and in years to come they would laugh about it but oh, how she wished he was with her now to take her in his arms and comfort her, dispelling the image of a tall, dark Spaniard and the touch of his mouth on hers.

Why hadn't Wade been in touch with her? She had written him a frantic letter almost begging him to phone her; surely he had received it. She sighed, dropping her head into her hands.

Suddenly, she jumped as if she had been struck. What a fool she was! At least she could talk to him. She lifted the receiver and dialled the operator, and in an unbelievably short time she heard the bell ringing in Spain. The receiver was lifted and Jan blinked; she had

30

taken it for granted that the operator would speak English.

'Do you speak English?' she asked hesitantly and was rewarded by a response in faultless English. She drew a breath of relief and asked if she could speak to Wade.

'I am not sure if Señor Felton is in the building.' The smooth answer shocked Jan: she had been so sure she would soon hear Wade's voice. 'I will see if I can find his location,' the woman said just in time to prevent Jan dropping the phone back on to its cradle. She cuddled the phone in her hands as if it were a lifeline. She was sure she would break down if she couldn't talk to someone about the awful thing that had happened, and who else was there but Wade? The phone came to life and the voice said that she had Señor Felton for her. Jan clasped the receiver, tears pouring down her face as she heard Wade's voice.

She could hardly speak but somehow it all came tumbling out.

'Why did you send me to take a message to Phillip Johnson?' she said at last.

'I don't know Phillip Johnson, though I have heard the name. He's a top executive, isn't he? Not my style at all. Oh, love, you have made a muddle. I sent the message to Pippa Johns, room four on the third floor. She's an old friend; I bumped into her on my last visit, and I wanted to ask her about her parents. I have caused you a lot of trouble, haven't I, Jan? But it should be all right now. The big man telephoned me only an hour ago and I cleared it up. Cheer up, love. It's all over. I don't like my fiancée so upset.'

'Do you think it is over, Wade? Did Señor del Raimondes believe you?'

'Sure he did. I must go now, love.' Wade's voice

sharpened. 'The bosses here don't like the lower orders having phone calls.'

'I understand,' Jan said dully, her happiness at Wade calling her his fiancée disappearing fast. 'I won't phone again.'

'Best not, love. I will write.' And before she could answer he had gone, only the dialling tone purring in the empty room.

Jan wandered over to the window. Wade had tried to reassure her, passing the whole thing off as a mistake, but there had been something that had rung false. He was a shade too lighthearted, and that business of the names ... They weren't unalike, but her hearing was sharp and she was sure she had never heard the name of Pippa Johns before. She pressed her hand to her aching head. Wade was so far away he couldn't know how deserted and alone she felt. As far as he was concerned the whole thing was a mix up on her part and something of a joke. He had done his best to clear matters up and perhaps he had; she just wished the whole thing was over and done with.

She was trying to face an uncertain future when the telephone rang.

'Miss Shelley.' The deep voice needed no introduction and Jan answered with the calmness of resignation.

'Yes, Señor del Raimondes.'

'You will come to number twelve, Bankview House at seven this evening without fail. Do not even think of not appearing, or you will regret it more than you can imagine.' It was an order, not a request, and Jan responded in like manner.

'I'll be there,' she said and put the receiver down.

For a short time relief overshadowed the dread at having to see him again. Until now she had been able to forget the way he had made her feel, the masterful kiss, the hardness of his body and the heat of his skin under her fingers; now she knew she would see him in a few hours her stomach curled into a tight knot and she didn't know how she would find strength to obey him.

By six o'clock she was ready in a simple pale grey dress that was quietly formal and, she hoped, suitable for the most difficult interview she had ever had to attend. She drew her Mini up in the forecourt of Bankview House at five minutes to seven. It was a new block of flats; Jan had never been inside but by all accounts it was as exclusive as it was expensive.

Number twelve proved to be on the top floor, and Jan thought that even the lift was out of the ordinary with its oak panelling and thick blue carpet. She stepped out into a hall with a heavy door at the end. There was only one flat on the floor, bringing home to her that Carlos del Raimondes was a very wealthy man. She looked for a bell push but, not finding one, raised her hand to knock as the door opened.

'Come in, Miss Shelley, I am glad to see you are punctual.' He seemed bigger than ever, his close-fitting sand-coloured trousers and cream shirt setting off his tanned complexion and his dark hair and eyes. His shirt was open at the neck and she noticed with fascination the dark curls of chest hair. He stepped slightly to one side, allowing her to enter, and Jan unavoidably brushed against him in the too narrow space. She saw his eyes gleam as her breasts and thighs came into contact with him and knew he had deliberately blocked her way.

The room she entered was large and filled with light from two huge windows that gave an entrancing view of the Derbyshire hills. In other circumstances she would have enjoyed it, but the man at her side overshadowed everything else. She stood a few feet away from him, her back to a wide fireplace, barely seeing the dark green carpet and deep crimson chairs, her attention wholly on what he was about to say.

'I have decided it would be a waste of your undoubted talents to have you sent to prison, but neither am I willing to continue to employ you,' he stated flatly.

Relief and resentment fought for pride of place in Jan's mind. 'I suppose I should thank you, but as I am not guilty I have nothing to be grateful for. I am at least thankful that I need never see you again and I can always get another job.'

'I think not, Miss Shelley. Work is difficult to find and, without a reference, practically impossible.'

Jan caught her breath in dismay; she hadn't thought he would withhold a reference.

'My work is well known, *señor* and there are people who will believe me.'

'Not when I have spoken to them. No one will employ you under the shadow of suspected theft, and my influence is far reaching.' His eyes were cold, and for the first time Jan knew she wasn't going to get out of the mess she was in.

'What do you expect me to do, *señor*? Or doesn't it concern you that you have just taken away my livelihood?'

'It concerns me, Miss Shelley, and I have a position you can fill.' He grasped her arms and pulled her slowly to him. 'A position you will fill very well.'

Jan pushed away from him with all her strength and he let her go, a slight smile on his lips. She fought for calmness. His touch wrought havoc with her senses and even though she was out of the circle of his arms, long

supple and very strong fingers fitted round her wrist like
a steel bracelet. He was playing with her as a fisherman
plays a fish, able to pull in his catch with a flick of his
wrist.

'What is this position you are offering me, *señor*?'

'Not offering, Miss Shelley. I am insisting you take it,
otherwise——' He looked at her with dark fathomless
eyes, reminding her once again of a bird of prey. She
tugged her wrist experimentally to no avail.

'What does this position entail, *señor*? You are going
to tell me?'

'The position is that of my mistress,' he said bluntly,
'and one for which I think you undeniably suitable.'

Jan's eyes widened to their fullest extent and she
closed her lips firmly. She wasn't going to give the
damned man the satisfaction of knowing he had shaken
her down to her toes. She glared at him with all the scorn
of which she was capable.

'Not a very good joke, *señor*, but perhaps you aren't
really aware of what you have said. English is a difficult
language unless you were born here.'

His eyes gleamed with acknowledgement of a good
answer but the shake of his head told her it had missed its
target.

'Or attended school and university here,' he said with
a sardonic twist of his lips. 'A good try, Jacinta, but you
know I am quite familiar with the English language and
I meant exactly what I said.'

Jan was afraid he had, but she didn't allow her dismay
to show as she answered him.

'I find your offer outrageous and the answer is no,'
she said firmly.

'It isn't an offer,' he said, his manner deceptively
mild. 'It is an order, unless you wish to spend the next
five years in prison.'

'Five years? Oh, come now, *señor*, you exaggerate,' Jan said quaking inwardly at the idea of five days in prison, let alone years.

'As a first offender you might get off more lightly here, but not in Spain, and as the offence is linked with the pottery there I could possibly have you extradited.'

'No, you wouldn't. For goodness' sake, *señor*, how can you do such a thing?'

'I am sure it won't be necessary. I shall take very good care of my mistress.'

Jan felt as if he had poured a bucket of icy water over her and the chill was seeping into her bones.

'I won't be your mistress, even if it does mean going to prison for something I haven't done.'

He tightened his grip round the wrist he still held and pulled her effortlessly to him. His black eyes held anger and he brought his mouth down on hers, his lips hard against her soft ones. After a minute his kiss changed, his mouth moving gently over hers in a seductive movement, impelling Jan to open her lips in response. He raised his head and laughed.

'Do you really expect me to believe you prefer prison to my kisses?'

'I haven't done anything I could go to prison for and you know it,' she said recklessly.

'Do I?'

'Yes. I spoke to Wade Felton yesterday and he said he had spoken to you, so you know it was just a stupid muddle over names.' She waited breathlessly for him to laugh and say he hadn't been serious about her acting as his mistress, but he continued to regard her with a cold cynical gaze.

'I give you full marks for trying,' he said slowly, 'but the conversation I had with Felton proves nothing, except that he is clear. I established that he was in Spain when the theft took place, while you were here and only too ready to take advantage of the confusion of names. I still think you have an accomplice, and the field is wide open.'

Jan felt as if she had fallen a great depth; she hadn't known until now how much she had counted on Wade's story clearing her name.

'Wade knows I wouldn't do such a thing. He ... we...' She faltered under the sharp gleam in his dark eyes.

'Yes, Miss Shelley? Are you trying to tell me you and Wade Felton are lovers, or are you trying to pin the blame on to him?'

'It's nothing to do with you if Wade and I are ...'

'Lovers? I disagree, it has everything to do with me.' He pushed her towards a chair. 'Sit down, my little mistress-to-be, and I will tell you just what I expect of you.'

Jan sank down into the chair. 'You needn't be explicit, señor, I know what a mistress's duties are.'

'Then you will be surprised when I tell you, you are quite wrong. I don't want you in my bed; the idea of making love to a thief revolts me.'

Jan sat in stunned silence. Just when she thought he was running true to form as another rich sensualist who would go to any lengths for a woman he fancied, he told her very plainly that he didn't want her. She lifted her chin until she could look at him squarely. Not for a moment would she let him suspect the blow to her pride his words had been.

'If you don't want me for the usual thing, then what do you want from me?'

'Your co-operation, for one thing. You will move into this flat and to everyone but ourselves you will be my mistress.'

'Why? You can't leave it there; I have to know the

reason. You do realise that my reputation will be ruined?'

'You should have thought about that before you conspired to steal,' he thundered. 'I don't have to give you a reason. Suffice it to say that I need a mistress for the next few weeks or perhaps months and that as soon as the necessity is past you will leave.

'You will have no need to worry about money while you are here. As long as you perform any duties I ask of you to my complete satisfaction I shall be generous, and anything I give you, you may keep. When you do go I will see you obtain a suitable position. I wouldn't like to think you had to resort to yet more criminal activities.'

He crossed one long leg over the other and Jan thought she had never seen a more powerful and vital man and never had she loathed anyone as she did Carlos del Raimondes.

'You have no choice, Jacinta,' he said. She hated to hear her name on his mocking tongue.

'I don't like it, *señor*, I think I would rather take my chance with the police.'

A naked devil looked out of his eyes before he lowered his lids but he failed to keep the iron out of his voice.

'You have no choice,' he said again. 'Prison, even for a short time, will enter your soul, and I will personally see you never get another worthwhile job.' Allowing her time to digest his words, he strolled to a side-table and poured brandy into two glasses.

'This will help make my proposition more palatable,' he said offering her one of the drinks. Jan waved the glass away.

'I hardly ever drink,' she said, although she would have drunk the whole bottle if it would have got her out of his reach. He raised his eyebrows sceptically and put the glass on a table at her side, sitting down opposite to her, his eyes on her white face. He swallowed his own drink and picked up a drawing. Jan saw without surprise that it was her butterfly design. It seemed unreal, as if it existed in another life. The girl who had painted butterflies and dandelions was a different person from the girl who was bound to the devil sitting on the other side of the coffee-table.

'This is excellent,' he said tapping her drawing with a long finger. 'It is for a plate, is it not? Did you intend there to be more of them?'

Such was the power of the man that Jan answered automatically, 'I thought four, or maybe six if they prove popular.' She came to herself and stretched out her hand. 'That is my property, señor. Please give it to me.'

'On the contrary, it is mine; you designed it during working hours, I believe.'

'Not entirely. I had the idea when I was at home.'

'You developed it at work, or Mr Hartley certainly believes you did.'

Jan sighed. Carlos del Raimondes wouldn't be satisfied until he had stripped her of everything she possessed.

'There is no reason why you shouldn't carry out your ideas for the rest of the plates on a freelance basis. I will treat this one in the same way and we shall both benefit.'

Jan's eyes brightened with the first spark of hope she had had since the morning she had been accused of stealing the glaze. At least he was willing to pay for her designs ... Or was he? Could it be just an extra inducement to get her to agree to his schemes?

'Are you going to pay me properly?' she asked, her cheeks burning as she saw the sardonic look in his eyes.

'Certainly I shall pay you, my mercenary mistress. I suggest ...' He mentioned a sum that Jan knew was fair and she nodded agreement.

'I will have the firm's solicitors draw up a contract and you can let it be known you are leaving to have more freedom in your work. That should take care of your precious reputation nicely.'

'Not if you flaunt me as your mistress, and that I take it is the point of the whole thing.'

'Intelligent as well as beautiful. You could be right, but we will have to see which way the cat walks.'

'Don't you mean in which direction the eagle flies?' Jan blurted out and she could have slapped herself when he laughed.

'So you see me as an eagle? If you meet my grandfather you will find there are two of us.'

'Shall I meet him?'

'Not if I can avoid it, but we can't always order events as we wish.'

He could and did; there wasn't much he couldn't do or anything or anyone he couldn't have if he really put his mind to it. She knew with a certainty she didn't question that Carlos del Raimondes was a man above other men, but that only made her hate him more.

'You may go home tonight; I will call for you at nine tomorrow morning. That will give you time to pack and give up your cottage. Your landlord won't mind, he can always let it to holidaymakers.'

'Tomorrow is too soon. You expect miracles, señor.'

'I expect only what I can command. You will start your duties as my mistress tomorrow evening and we have much to do before then to fit you for your new position.' The arrogance in his tone and the way he looked at her, letting his eyes take in every detail of her modestly priced dress and chain-store shoes made Jan see red.

'You will have to take me as you find me,' she

snapped. 'I have neither the inclination or the money to make myself over to your ideas.'

'You begin to bore me, Jacinta. The money for your requirements is my business, and before you throw your glass at my head may I remind you that you will do well to obey me. You can think of anything I provide as the uniform for the job, and you may be sure I shall get my money's worth. It is also time you called me Carlos; my mistresses always do.'

Jan returned home, walking out of the building and getting into her car as if she were a mechanical doll. She looked round her familiar sitting-room and it was as if she had been away for days instead of barely two hours. How could she do what that devil commanded? What would Wade think when he heard, as he would sooner or later? Her story of wanting to work at home wasn't a very good one. More than ever she needed to see and speak to Wade in person, not at the end of a telephone. A slight uneasiness prickled her skin. Wade could be very persuasive when he liked; surely he could have convinced Carlos del Raimondes of her innocence. She shrugged her doubts away. Wade had done all he could, but Carlos del Raimondes was impervious to persuasion.

The bell gave its harsh buzz and Jan ran to the door, so convinced after her sleepless night that he would have changed his mind that she smiled at him. The man standing before her blinked then smiled back, and Jan took a step backwards. Once before he had smiled in a fashion she didn't like and now he was doing it again, but this smile was a seductive response to an invitation she hadn't given. Jan frowned and tilted her chin proudly.

He followed her into the cottage and, standing in the

middle of the living-room, gazed round.

'Adequate,' he murmured, 'but not the right setting for you, Jacinta. Your beauty deserves a better frame.'

Jan glared at him. How dared he criticise her home?

'You have come to tell me you have changed your mind, *señor*,' she said stiffly. 'I am sure you realise your plan won't work. I have thought deeply over the whole matter and you must believe I had nothing to do with the theft.'

'So you still won't admit your guilt,' he said interestedly, his eyes on her mouth.

Jan blushed and looked past him.

'I can't confess to something of which I am innocent, even you must see that, and if you are still convinced of my guilt I can't believe it would help you to have me sent to prison.'

'Neither do I, and we have already agreed on the form my compensation will take, have we not?' He lifted an eyebrow enquiringly.

'It's a stupid plan *señor*. We should have to pretend to be fond of each other, but we both know that neither of us can bear to touch the other.'

'Oh, more than friendly, I think, unless you prefer to play the part of a gold digger.'

Jan gasped. 'I would not.'

'No, and I won't pretend to be a besotted sugar daddy, so there is only one way we can be convincing.'

'What's that?' Jan asked cautiously. She didn't trust him an inch.

'We shall have to convince anyone interested that we are in love.'

'Not possible. I couldn't pretend to be in love with you for a million pounds. I would rather love a snake.' Anger flashed into his eyes and for a moment Jan thought he would strike her, then he laughed.

'Snakes are very popular with some people,' he said.

'Not with me, they make me shudder.'

'You will have to control your emotions, Jacinta.' He laughed again and Jan wished for a second time that they were two ordinary people who were attracted to each other. She wrinkled her nose; he wasn't an ordinary man by any stretch of the imagination and millionaires weren't in her social circle, so the chances of meeting him socially would have been almost nil. It had taken an earthquake to bring them together.

'At least I shan't be bored with you as my mistress,' he said, the laughter still lingering in his eyes. Jan closed her eyes briefly; bored was the last thing she would be, either. She fought against an impulse to touch him, shivering as her imagination took off, giving her a picture of Carlos as her real lover. A picture of them lying naked together came vividly into her mind, so vividly she felt her face grow hot and was only brought back to the present by his amused, 'What has made you blush, Jacinta?' which she steadfastly ignored.

'Come, we have a lot do do.' He put his hand under her elbow and turned to the door.

'Wait, señor, I haven't packed.'

He brought his eyebrows together in a frown. 'Surely you have had time enough? But it is of no importance. I will provide you with a new wardrobe and everything else you can possibly want.' Jan started to protest, but he lifted a large shapely hand.

'You must realise, my dearest Jacinta, that none of your clothes are suitable for your new position.' His dark eyes roved contemptuously over her grey trouser suit.

'I dislike women in trousers unless they are indulging in sports that require them and you will wear clothes of good quality at all times.'

Jan's eyes flashed with anger and she flung her head back. 'That's tough, because I refuse to wear anything you provide.'

His face darkened and he pulled her out of the cottage, banged the door behind them, took her key from her hand, locked the door and pushed her into the passenger seat of a long silvery green sports car. Jan tried to open the door but he slid behind the wheel and pressed a button on the dashboard; Jan heard her lock click smoothly into place.

She glared at him, her violet eyes dark and stormy.

'I don't know what you are playing at, *señor*, but I can't just abandon everything I own. It may not seem worth much to you but it's all I have and some of the things were left to me by my parents and I value them.'

'I realise that, Jacinta, and I will see that everything, including giving up the cottage, is taken care of.'

'I don't want to give my home up. This "position" of yours is for only a few weeks, isn't it? I shall need somewhere to live afterwards.'

He started the car, ignoring her protests, they travelled for some time before either spoke again. They joined the motorway for London and he raised an eyebrow at her continued silence.

'Aren't you going to ask our destination?' he asked.

'Why should I? It won't make any difference if I don't approve, will it?'

'No, Jacinta. Neither will it help either of us if you sulk all the way.'

'I am not sulking.' Jan sat upright.

'Yes, you are, and I don't find it at all attractive. You are a grown woman, not a child. We have agreed you are to act the part of my mistress and I won't tolerate behaviour that will ruin everything before we have started. To look at you no one would believe that you even like me, let alone spend your nights in my bed making passionate love.'

Jan moved uneasily in her seat. His mocking voice brought her to the edge of tears and she turned her face away, staring blindly at the fields and neat farms they were passing. She wanted to scream at him, tell him how much she hated him, but to give way would only plunge her deeper into despair. She needed all her wits about her if she was to come out of this awful situation intact in mind and body. She wouldn't become his mistress; that would destroy her completely. She was already attracted to him, much against her will, and although he said he was repulsed by her she suspected that wasn't true.

She stared out of the window without seeing anything, unconsciously stiffening her spine and holding her head high, a gesture not missed by the man at her side. What was she doing? Even to think she was attracted to Carlos was nonsense, and dangerous nonsense at that. He was the kind of man who would attract nearly every woman he met, and unfortunately she was going to be in close proximity to him for weeks. She would have to be on her guard every moment they were together.

She glanced at him from the corner of her eye; he would be very hard to resist if he really wanted a woman. Jan stifled a pang of regret and one of remorse that she should think of any man but Wade in such a way. It was the strain of the last few days that had caused her thoughts to go astray. There was only one man for her, and it wasn't Carlos del Raimondes. She forced herself to pay attention to the scenery until they drew up before a service station.

* * *

Several hours later Jan followed Carlos into a small hotel. She waited while he registered and received a key from the young man behind the reception desk and then went with him docilely as, grasping her arm, he led her into the lift on the heels of the porter laden with the boxes and parcels she had acquired. There were so many of them she had lost count before Carlos was half-way through selecting the clothes he thought she should have, and by the time he was satisfied she was exhausted.

At the beginning of the shopping marathon she had tried to argue, but one sardonic glance from his dark eyes taught her the futility of disagreeing with him.

'I know this isn't where you usually buy your clothes, Jacinta,' he said in a voice smooth as polished marble. He waved his hand round the private room of the exclusive London fashion house. 'I am sure you would prefer to shop in a multiple store, but you wouldn't find anything suitable for our purpose there.'

'Your purpose, I think you mean,' Jan said through clenched teeth. 'For your information, I would not prefer a large store, but my pocket dictates where I shop.'

'Then you are doubly fortunate that now your preference and my pocket coincide.'

Jan drew her breath in sharply. He was, without doubt, the most arrogant, self-opinionated man she had ever come across. She realised with a stab of horror that she had said the words out loud, and was rewarded by a lift of his eyebrows and a sarcastic curl of the well-shaped mouth.

'You are entitled to your opinion, as long as you don't voice it in front of other people. We are lovers, remember?'

'Only pretend lovers,' Jan said, anger making her eyes sparkle.

'True.' He turned to greet the woman who came towards them.

'Wake up, Jacinta.' Carlos pushed her gently into a chair in a sitting-room decorated in brown and gold, thanked the porter and handed him what, by the grin on the man's face, was a lavish tip. 'We will stay here for a few days and finish our shopping in comfort.' He rested a hand on the arm of her chair and Jan wished he wouldn't stand over her. He was so big and powerful she felt threatened. He pulled her to her feet.

'You are falling asleep where you sit; you would be better off in bed.' He opened a door to reveal a lavishly appointed bedroom. Jan looked at the king-sized bed and felt the colour steal into her cheeks.

Carlos looked at her, his eyes hooded.

'Don't worry. There are two bedrooms, though we can share this one if you prefer.' He looked at her, his eyes dark and slumbrous, and a strange tension flashed between them. Jan threw up her head like a small animal who senses a hunter high above and stared back at him, willing herself not to tremble.

'No, thank you *señor*, I like to sleep alone.'

'I could teach you otherwise.'

'I would make a very bad pupil, and you are forgetting that only a few days ago you couldn't bear to touch me.'

'You are right to remind me. When I look at your lovely face and your body that is made for a man's delight I forget that the real you is a despicable little tramp.'

Jan drew her breath in harshly. If she hadn't been so tired she would have hit him—but he would only hit her back, she thought ruefully.

'I am grateful for small mercies,' she snapped. 'I can't think of anything worse than the honour of sharing your

bed, and now, if you will excuse me . . .' A hand on her
arm stopped her as she would have entered the bedroom
with the firm intention of shutting him out. She tilted
her head enquiringly and not a little apprehensively. He
smiled and drew her attention to the tray which a maid
in a smart brown uniform was placing on a coffee-table.

'You will rest better for some refreshment and the
maid will unpack for you while we drink.'

Jan was very tempted. She was thirsty and tired and
the thought of a refreshing cup of tea while someone else
did the work was irresistible. She sat down and, under
Carlos's approving gaze, lifted the milk jug and looked at
him.

'Milk, but no sugar, please. I acquired the habit of
afternoon tea during my years in England and I find the
sight of a pretty English girl presiding over the tea-tray a
pleasing picture, one I shall continue to enjoy wherever I
am.'

Jan thanked him as he passed her the plate of cakes.
She would never get used to Carlos's change of moods.
One minute he was calling her names that made her
seethe and the next he was relaxed, talking easily as if
they were friends. They chatted about London as they
sipped the fragrant tea and ate cream cakes and she
wasn't really surprised to find that he knew far more
about the city than she did. Forgetting that she hated
him and the position he had forced her into, she leaned
nearer to him, her eyes shining as she listened to him
describing the places they would visit during their stay.

She was brought out of her dream of visiting the
Tower and seeing the Crown Jewels by Carlos looking at
his watch.

'It is time for you to rest, Jacinta. We are dining out

and will possibly run into some of my friends; I want you to look your best. It would never do if anyone we might meet thinks I have a poor taste in mistresses,' he said scathingly. He held her chair for her and Jan, back to the unwelcome present, walked past him into the bedroom.

She slipped off her shoes and dress and lay down on the bed. She was very tired but thoughts of Carlos came between her and sleep and, stripped of the euphoria he had woven with his stories of old London, they were painful ones. How could she have got into such a mess? It went against all her principles even to pretend to be a man's mistress. Aunt Mary would have been horrified, but it was only pretence, she assured herself, ignoring the small voice that said Carlos wanted it to be reality and what Carlos del Raimondes wanted he always got.

CHAPTER FOUR

SHE was awakened by a touch, light as a feather, on her nose. She opened her eyes and gasped as Carlos kissed her again, this time on her mouth. She sat up and pushed him away and he straightened up, chuckling at her startled expression.

'I couldn't resist you. You look so delectable lying there half naked.'

Jan's hands flew to her breast, exposed above the lace of her slip. Carlos chuckled again and, slipping one hand under her waist, pulled her off the bed with an ease that made Jan aware of how very strong he was. He brought her close to him and tilted her face up to his.

'You are so tempting with the drowsiness of sleep in your lovely eyes and your spun silver hair loosened from the tight knot you have worn it in all day.'

Jan struggled to be free. She was still half asleep but warning bells were ringing furiously. He was looking at her with an intensity she was afraid wasn't just friendly. What had happened to his resolve not to touch her? The whole situation was getting out of hand. She pushed her hands between them as his lips caressed hers, sending electric shocks running through her. He cupped her head with one hand and she was unable to escape lips that tantalised briefly before his kiss changed and deepened. He invaded her mouth like a Spanish *conquistador*, taking everything he wanted. She closed her eyes in surrender as he explored the inner moistness, her arms curled round his neck, and she melted against him, her legs unable to support her.

He moved swiftly and Jan was lying on the bed with his weight half over her before she could murmur a protest. His fingers trespassed, pulling down the shoulder straps of her slip. Brought out of her trance by his hands peeling her clothes from her until she was only left with flimsy satin briefs, Jan tried to cover herself. She pushed her hands against his broad shoulders in vain. He was far too strong and there was nothing she could do to prevent him making love to her. She looked into the depths of his dark eyes and a sob escaped her.

'Don't, Carlos, you promised. You think I'm a thief. How can a man of your supposed integrity discard your principles to such an extent?' she said with all the scorn she could muster. He released her slowly, his eyes on her flushed face before travelling slowly downwards, and she became only too aware of how taut her breasts were, the nipples hardened into buds. She flushed and tried to pull the sheet over her but he flicked it away and glared at her, sending a shiver rippling over her sensitive skin.

'I ask myself that every time I see you, and I can only think that something in me demands revenge,' he said harshly. 'Again you have to remind me that you are beneath my notice. I must be mad to want to lay one finger on you, let alone make love to you, but I can't promise it won't happen one day. When I am ready I will take you, but now there are more urgent matters. I will give you fifteen minutes to get ready for dinner and if you are not ready I will dress you myself. Wear something suitable to your present position.' He walked out and Jan stared at the door, wishing she had a pot of boiling oil or something similar to wipe the confident look from his face.

He would take her when he was ready, would he? Not

if she had any say in the matter. Jan rolled off the bed,
rushed into into the bathroom and turned on the shower.
Fifteen minutes, he had said, and if she wasn't ready he
would play lady's maid. He would be an expert at the
job, she was sure, but she wasn't going to risk finding
out just how good he was.

She rubbed herself dry with a large gold towel and lost
no time on getting into a lacy bra and panties. She drew
cobwebby tights over her slender legs and, standing
before the wardrobe, looked at the dresses hanging there.
For a moment she contemplated disobeying him and
choosing something unsuitable, but the small spurt of
rebellion died as she thought of his anger. She stretched
out a hand and selected a heavy crêpe dinner dress in a
violet that matched her eyes and hastily pulled it on.

Clothes, good clothes, did make a difference. Jan
looked at her reflection, her eyes round with astonishment. She had had her hair styled and it had been cut
and shaped, leaving it long enough to swirl up on top of
her head in the way she now wore it. She touched the
curls framing her face; they seemed to take on a special
gleam against the deep colour of her dress. It was simply
cut with a low neckline that hinted at the curve of her
breasts. The sleeves, full to the elbow, were gathered
into velvet bands repeated at the narrow waist, and the
skirt was slightly gathered, falling gracefully to mid calf.
High-heeled sandals that were little more than violet
wisps completed the picture.

'That dress is very elegant; it makes you look
sophisticated.' Carlos's deep voice made her swing
round and she caught her breath at how marvellous he
looked in his well cut dinner jacket.

'Isn't that how you want me to look?'

'I am not sure. It is severe, and with your hair like that
I should think you a schoolmistress except for your eyes

and your mouth which send out invitations no man could resist'. His eyes travelled downwards and Jan felt her nipples harden, thrusting against her dress. He laughed, devils springing to life in his dark eyes.

'I have decided it will do very well: cool deep water outside for everyone to see and fire underneath for my private delight. All you need is a finishing touch.' He turned her round again and her eyes flew to the mirror as she felt something cold slide round her neck.

'Do you like it?' Carlos asked as she stared at the diamonds set in delicate gold hanging from a fine gold chain.

'It is very beautiful and I am sure it was very expensive but I won't wear it.' Her hands went to the back of her neck but he prevented her from touching the catch.

'Why not? You like it. I saw the expression in your eyes before you decided to refuse it.'

'I may be playing the part of your mistress and forced to wear the clothes you provide but I won't wear valuable jewellery.'

'You will, Jacinta. It is part of our agreement that you accept anything I give you. What would my friends think of me if I didn't provide my latest mistress with jewels?' He touched the pendant with a long finger, allowing it to linger on her breast. 'It is not worth as much as you would have made by selling my secrets, but you have still gained considerably.'

'I don't want to gain anything! I didn't steal your wretched glaze and I won't take anything I haven't worked for.'

'That can be arranged,' he murmured softly, and Jan closed her eyes against the flame that leapt to life in his. She could feel it, too, the longing to be in his arms, to have his hard body pressed to hers, to run her hands over his skin. She opened her eyes and met his in the mirror. Dear God, he knew exactly what she was thinking.

His expression changed to one of deep contempt.

'*Diablo*! I must be out of my mind. How can I even think of touching you? You are an immoral little thief and all I can think of is how soft your skin is and how you will respond when we make love.'

'As you say, you are mad to think of such a thing and you can be very sure I would not respond to you in any way.' Jan tilted her chin up, meeting his eyes. 'You are my employer, even though the job is unconventional, but that is all you are.'

'I could be much more, as I think you know.'

'I know nothing of the kind. What you are suggesting would only be acceptable if we loved each other, and I am sure you agree that whatever we feel for each other, it is very far from love.'

'You are right, Jacinta, it is not love, but I believe desire and the satisfaction and pleasure it can bring are far superior to the emotion you call love. That romantic nonsense is for teenagers and I am long past that uncomfortable age.' He picked up the short velvet cloak that went with her dress and placed it round her shoulders.

'We will go out to dinner now. Remember you are my mistress and act as if you loved me to distraction. I will not tolerate you flirting with anyone we may meet. You will wear the pendant, Jacinta. Don't try to go against me or you will find, to your sorrow, that I can be a very hard master.'

The first part of the evening turned out better than Jan had thought possible. They dined in what she recognised as one of London's most famous restaurants and she exclaimed with delight at the view of the Thames she could see from her seat in the wide window.

The meal was delicious and Jan remembered for a long time the duckling in its special sauce and the mixture of fruit, cream and liqueur which ended the meal. Carlos looked up from the cheese he was eating and smiled.

'You are enjoying your evening after all. I am not such an ogre, no?'

'No,' Jan agreed warily. At that moment she could almost forget the threats he had uttered only a short time ago. Carlos, as he was now, was a different person from the grim-faced man set on a preposterous course.

'You are coming to terms with your position, mm?' he asked, and all at once Jan felt afraid. There had been something in his tone that had been neither friendly nor comforting.

She put her spoon down—she had completely lost her appetite for her sweet—and looked into dark eyes that saw too much and demanded more than she was willing to give.

'I don't think I shall ever be reconciled with living a lie, señor. I was brought up to be truthful.' His eyes narrowed and he grasped her hands as it lay on the table.

'It may not always be a lie. Propinquity may even make me forget what a worthless woman you are and remember only the wild-rose colour in your cheeks and the way you melt against me,' he sneered.

'Do not trouble yourself, señor. I am quite content to be unworthy of sharing your bed; in fact, I prefer it that way.' She jerked her hand back but he increased his grip until she could have cried out with pain.

'I shall not tell you again, Jacinta, to call me Carlos. What kind of fools do you think we shall look if you continue to address me so formally? Say it, Jacinta, it is an easy name.' His dark eyes compelled obedience and she swallowed nervously and stammered 'Carlos'.

'It was easy, was it not? And now is your chance to practise.' He stood up as a tall, dark woman followed by an equally dark man came towards them.

'Carlos, darling, I couldn't believe it was you. I thought you were in Spain.' The woman flung her arms round him and kissed him lingeringly and Carlos kissed her back with equal enthusiasm. The dark man frowned and a flash of almost physical pain made Jan clench her teeth together. She couldn't understand why the sight of Carlos kissing someone else should disturb her so much. She couldn't be jealous of this overblown peony of a woman. No, of course she couldn't. You had to love, or at least feel some affection, to be jealous and the only feeling she had for Carlos was hatred.

'Jacinta, may I introduce Señor and Señora Bennueto. Rosalba, Pedro, this is Jacinta Shelley, a close friend of mine who until recently worked at my pottery here in England.' Jan felt a blush creep over her cheeks; the emphasis Carlos had put on 'a close friend' had made their relationship only too clear. Rosalba hadn't missed a thing, and the look she cast at Jan held sheer venom. They chatted for a few minutes, then Pedro Bennueto took his wife's arm.

'We must go. I will bid you goodnight, Carlos, Miss Shelley.' His wife murmured her goodnights and, on the point of departure, added silkily, 'So nice to have met you, Miss Shelley. Carlos, Alva will be interested to hear you are not lonely without her.' She swept out of the restaurant and Jan could almost hear the trumpets' triumphant call.

'I don't begin to understand that last bit, Carlos, but I

think your dear friend is poison.'

'She is, and you will soon understand what she was talking about. It will only take as long as a letter or perhaps a telephone call to Spain.' The last words were uttered so angrily that Jan looked at him apprehensively. Carlos took a deep breath and picked up his wine glass.

'We will forget my friends and enjoy our evening. Drink your wine and we will go somewhere we can dance. That is a good idea, no?'

Jan shook her head. She didn't think it was a good idea. She wanted nothing more than to be held close in his arms while they danced to a romantic tune; she longed for the scent of his masculinity in her nostrils and the sight of strong features near to hers. She gasped. What was she thinking of? It was in Wade's arms she longed to be, with Wade's fair-skinned face next to hers. How could she be so disloyal, even in her thoughts? She stroked her ring finger. Carlos's eyes narrowed intently and she dropped her hands to her lap.

'If you don't mind, Carlos, I would rather go back to the hotel. It has been a long day.' He cast her an enigmatic glance that told her nothing but he did as she asked, and in a very short time they were back in the sitting-room of their suite.

'Shall I send for coffee?' Carlos asked as he helped her off with her cloak, his hands brushing her skin as he lifted it away from her shoulders.

'No, thank you. I am tired and will say goodnight.' She walked away from him but he strode between her and the door.

'You wouldn't leave without saying goodnight properly, would you? And are you sure you want to say it at all? This way you won't have to tell lies.'

'To do as you wish would be a bigger lie. We don't

love each other and sexual gratification wouldn't be enough for me, even if it would for you.'

He laughed harshly. 'You don't know what you are saying, Jacinta. What kind of lovers have you had? I can assure you I will be enough for you in every way.'

'I have no wish to test your statement, Carlos. Now, I really am very tired.' She moved towards the door and he stepped back, his face hard and cold, his mouth set in a straight line.

'I will let you go now, but do not count on my indulgence for much longer, Jacinta. I am not noted for my patience.'

They drove back to Derbyshire the next morning, Carlos having decided overnight that nothing was to be gained by staying in the capital any longer. Jan sat silently beside him and wished she could put the clock back to the day she had gone to Birmingham. But would anything have turned out differently? She looked at the strong, determined face of the man beside her and knew it wouldn't. What Carlos wanted, he got, and she just happened to fit his requirements. No, not in every way, not yet, but his words of the night before told her he intended her to share his bed before much longer.

Jan drew her brows together in a puzzled frown. He didn't love her, didn't even like her. He was having to fight against his better instincts, and she hadn't thought he was a man who would let his desires rules him or who would change his mind about something like this. Perhaps he was beginning to believe her. A wild hope shot through her, but one glimpse of his hard, cold face quenched her rising spirits. No, this man wouldn't take her word for anything; only cast-iron proof would make him change his mind.

The mystery of his about-face still remained and, try

as she might, Jan couldn't resolve it, unless making love to her in the face of her continued refusals and his own reluctance was a challenge he couldn't resist, and so unimportant to him that it wouldn't touch the real man at all. She set her jaw firmly; it wasn't going to happen. She didn't intend to lie in any man's bed unless they loved each other.

'Why are you looking as if an enemy were at your gates, Jacinta?' His eyes flicked to her face, taking in her determined expression before he gave his attention back to the road.

'You are mistaken, why should I feel threatened.'

'With very good reason. I am sure you remember our conversation before you went to your lonely bed last night.'

Jan stifled an exclamation. He seemed to know her every thought; she would have to guard them closely in future. 'I have forgotten what we talked about last night, Carlos, so it can't have been important, can it?' He chuckled but, far from being reassuring, it made Jan want to open the door and run, not a good idea at seventy miles an hour.

'You have not forgotten one word, Jacinta, but it pleases you to play games and it pleases me to indulge you for a short time.' He lapsed into silence and Jan was more than thankful when he pulled up before Bankview House. He sat looking at the building for some time before getting out and once they were in the penthouse he walked from room to room frowning thoughtfully, finally standing with his back to the window, his arms folded across his chest, his eyes hooded. All at once he seemed to make up his mind and he made for the telephone with impatient strides.

He tapped his fingers on the table while he waited to

be answered and Jan was surprised to hear he was talking to an estate agent and even more surprised when Carlos proceeded to give details of a house he wanted to view.

'Nonsense,' he said after a moment. 'You must have something to suit me. I will give you half an hour. Please ring back. Stupid man,' he said, putting the receiver down. 'He said he hadn't got a house with more than four bedrooms when I saw one advertised in last night's paper under their name that had eight.' He grinned at Jan's puzzled expression. 'I have decided a house will suit me better than this flat. I may need more space in the near future.' He looked round the huge room, which seemed to shrink to half its size.

'More room for two of us? You must be mad! This place is enormous.'

'I need room to breathe and I would like a garden, and a wife or a mistress needs the right setting, as I am sure you agree.'

The phone ringing prevented her answering him. Carlos picked up the receiver and barked 'del Raimondes' and listened intently. Jan got to her feet. However fast the agent was in finding a house, they would have to remain here for the present and by the time Carlos did move, the reason for her being here would have vanished and she could leave. Meanwhile she would start to unpack. The sound as Carlos replaced the receiver and his impatient call brought her back into the room before she had got very far.

'There are three houses that could be suitable; we are to pick up the keys at the agent's office. We will go now. You can unpack later.'

'I didn't think estate agents worked on Sundays,' she said as they drew up before a small office.

'I rang him at his home and someone will be here.'
Carlos opened his door as a small blue car came to a stop
with a squeal of brakes. A young man jumped out and
produced forms and keys. Carlos thanked him and the
young man watched as they drove away.

'He looks as if a hurricane has hit him,' Jan said. 'Do
you push everyone you meet about like that? I thought it
was only me you treated so ruthlessly.'

'I don't believe in wasting time,' Carlos said stiffly
and for a moment Jan thought he was hurt by her
criticism. She dismissed the idea immediately. He
wasn't the kind of man to be affected by her; he was
complete in himself and didn't need anyone's good
opinions.

The first house was Victorian, large and rather ugly,
set in prim gardens that made Jan long to throw out all
the bedding plants and replace them with shrubs that
might go a little way towards softening the bleak
building. Carlos walked through it rapidly, muttering
under his breath, then, to Jan's surprise, went over it
again. She followed him, taking in every unattractive
feature. The house could be lived in, the decorations
weren't bad, but it was filthy and cold, even on a day as
warm as this one. Jan looked round the lofty rooms, it
didn't appear as if there was any central heating.

'This house is possible,' Carlos said with a keen-eyed
glance at Jan. 'Don't you agree that if it were thoroughly
cleaned and with fires roaring in every room it would be
very cosy in winter?' He glanced at Jan's slim white
hands tipped with shining pink-varnished nails.

'It would never be cosy. It would require fires even in
the height of summer,' she snapped, fighting an urge to
put her hands behind her. Surely he didn't expect her to
scrub paintwork and floors and light all the fires he was

talking about? She met his eyes and knew that was just what he did expect.

'I think it could be made very pleasant.' He turned away from her to inspect the enormous fireplace.

It would need a lot of work to get clean, let alone make it shine, and Jan dared not think of the amount of fuel it would take. Her shoulders ached with just the thought of the buckets and buckets of coal she would have to carry.

'If I had the time to spare for you to get it in order I would seriously consider it, but unfortunately I want to move in quickly so, reluctantly, we must look elsewhere. I am sure you are as disappointed as I am, *querida*, but it would all take too long.' He waved his hand round the room, dismissing the house and its problems, and Jan drew a sigh of relief.

'I hope the other two are in better condition,' he growled as they drove towards the next address on his list.

'Don't lose heart, Carlos, you have only just started looking. It could take months.' Jan wanted to laugh at his disgruntled expression. He would have delighted in the work that awful house would have meant for her. She turned her head to the window. There was nothing to laugh at; he intended to get his money's worth out of her in one way or the other and if she wouldn't sleep with him then he would work her to death.

'I haven't got months; I wish to move at once.' He came to a stop and sat looking at the house in front of them.

'Oh, I like this one, Carlos,' Jan said, gazing at the long, low converted farmhouse.

'Mm, do you? Get out, Jacinta, and we will go in.' Ten minutes later they were back in the car and Jan was feeling disappointed. It was obvious it wasn't what

Carlos wanted and she had to admit that the interior didn't live up to the promise of the outside. The rooms were small and rather dark and the kitchen needed replanning, and although those things could be remedied, the farm building in full view of the sitting-room could not.

'I don't like silos practically in the garden,' Carlos said. 'I know you like the house but it won't do.'

'I realise that, and it's really not my business. It's your choice, Carlos.'

'Yours as well. A man is a fool if he doesn't try to please his woman.'

Jan drew as far away from him as the car would allow. 'I shall be with you for a short time only, so my views don't matter.'

Carlos slanted a look at her out of hooded eyes and turned down a long drive lined on either side with flowering shrubs. Jan forgot she was annoyed as they negotiated a bend in the drive and a house came into view.

'Oh, how lovely!' She looked her fill at the small Georgian manor house as Carlos halted the car in front of a long flight of steps. It was built of stone that had taken on a mellowness over the years, adding to its beauty. The perfectly proportioned windows gleamed in the sunlight and stone tubs overflowing with flowers gave an extra touch of elegance. The background of trees and shrubs enhanced its dignity and Carlos murmured in satisfaction.

'This is what I have been looking for. Let us hope it's as good inside.' He opened the door with a large brass key and smiled as they entered a large, square hall.

CHAPTER FIVE

Two hours later Carlos closed the door behind them and turned to Jan.

'I shall buy this house. I am right in thinking you like it as much as I do?'

'It's perfect. I love it.'

'Perfect? Hardly. It needs refurnishing, the decorations are dreadful and the curtains are deplorable.'

'There are some lovely pieces of furniture, and when I said it was perfect I meant the shape and proportions of the rooms. And you must admit the gardens leave nothing to be desired.'

'From the little we have seen of them I think you are right,' Carlos said, looking at the catalogue in his hand. 'There are twenty-two acres of parkland, woods and gardens plus three farms let to tenants. Yes, this is what I want. I will put things in hand at once, and as I shall be busy you are in charge of decorating and refurnishing Over Grange.' He looked at her challengingly and Jan sighed.

'If you say so, but how do you know you will like my choice? I could be too extravagant.'

Carlos raised his eyebrows. 'You will have no chance to spend too much. You are an artist and I trust you not to spoil the house, but in every other way I only trust you when you are under my eye.'

Jan flushed painfully. She twisted her hands together and tried to ignore his remarks; it wouldn't help to protest her innocence again.

'The house isn't yours yet,' she said slowly. Carlos might not trust her but he was also going too fast, binding her to him so tightly that she wondered if she would ever be free—and knew with a feeling of fatality that he would keep her with him until he had no further use for her. She also knew, and fought the knowledge, that part of her didn't want to be free.

Carlos put her in the car and fastened her seatbelt.

'I have made up my mind to have it as one day I shall have you.' He started the car and in a surprisingly short time they arrived back at the flat and Carlos immediately phoned the estate agent. Twenty minutes later he came into the kitchen where Jan had just made coffee.

'The house is as good as mine, Jacinta. I am seeing the lawyers tomorrow and I hope to be in possession by the end of the week.'

'You can't buy a house as quickly as that,' Jan said.

'I can, Jacinta. Money can smooth many paths.'

He sat on the corner of the kitchen table, one long leg planted firmly on the floor, the other negligently swinging free, and she thought that there wasn't much he wouldn't be able to do or possess if he really wanted it badly enough. He wore casual slacks in cinnamon brown, a cream silk shirt open at the throat emphasising his broad shoulders. She tore her eyes away from the challenge in his and gave him a mug of coffee. She flinched as his warm fingers closed over hers and a faint smile curved his lips.

'I don't bite, Jacinta, yet you quiver every time I touch you.'

'Distaste,' Jan said curtly. 'I don't like you touching me.'

'It isn't wise for you to issue such a challenge, unless you are willing to face the consequences.' He laughed at the look on her face and the way she buried her nose in her mug, her hair falling forward, screening the faint blush that stained her delicate skin.

'I wasn't doing anything of the sort,' she said as soon as she could speak without screaming that he was a conceited chauvinist with only one idea in his head.

'Your very existence is a challenge,' Carlos said simply. 'You don't need to try; I can't be near you without wanting you.' He held her eyes with his, compelling her not to move. 'I want you in my bed beneath me, I want to run my hands slowly, very slowly over every inch of your white skin. I want to kiss you until you moan deep in your throat, to bury my face in the moonbeams that do duty for your hair. I want you to open to me and I want to fill you until you beg for more. Do not doubt for one moment that it will happen. I shall possess you completely so that no other man can ever take my place.'

His voice was husky and mesmerising, and not until it ceased did Jan come out of her trance. She shook her head to clear her brain. Never had any man said anything like that to her before and she didn't know what to do or say.

'You haven't heard words like that before?' he said, and Jan felt a spurt of anger at Carlos again reading her thoughts.

'No, and I hope I never do again. I can't stop you thinking what you will, but I don't want to know.' She faltered to a stop at the look in his dark eyes.

'It is too late, Jacinta, you know exactly how I feel. But why are you so outraged? Your lovers must have said such things to you.'

'Never. I wouldn't have listened,' she said, her eyes blazing with fury.

'You listened to me, and every time we exchange glances you will know what I am thinking,' he pointed out and Jan felt her face flame as the things he had said really penetrated.

'It makes no difference, Carlos. I will not sleep with you.'

'I don't think we would sleep, but you needn't fear for your virtue yet. I have to get over my distaste of making love to a thief and to forget seeing you gloat over the money in my wallet, but one day——' He left the words hanging in the air and Jan thought of swords suspended above her head by a single thread. He put his mug down.

'Get unpacked, Jacinta. I have work to do and from tomorrow we shall both be busy.'

The next two weeks were indeed busy. Jan found herself heavily involved with decorators and cleaners. She went with Carlos to London and they searched for carpets and curtains, and she learned to appreciate being able to order anything she wanted. Carlos was only impatient with her when she hesitated over the cost.

'The money isn't important,' he said. 'I wish you to order anything that will perfect the house.' He waited impatiently, drumming his fingers on the arm of a rosewood chair while Jan decided which colours would best blend together. She looked at him and wondered why he had accompanied her if he disliked shopping so much. She sighed. They had only just started; it would take hours yet.

It did take hours, and by the time they reached the china department Jan had had enough of Carlos's brooding presence. She chose tea and dinner services as quickly as she could, suppressing her desire to linger, but while Carlos signed a cheque for an amount that horrified her, she wandered to a display of china figures.

They were exquisite and would look lovely in the drawing-room. She stole a look at Carlos to see him frowning at her, so, casting one last glance at the lovely figure of Autumn and touching the sheaf of corn she carried with a gentle fingertip, she started to join him, but to her surprise he strolled over to her.

'So that is what has caught your attention. Very pretty,' he said in so bored a tone that Jan walked briskly out of the store and didn't speak again until they were in the car on the way back to Over Grange.

'Why did you come shopping with me? You were bored out of your mind. I could have managed perfectly well on my own.'

'I must confess traipsing round shops is not my scene,' he drawled. 'I much prefer the finished article, in this case a fully furnished house, but you forget I had to sign the cheques.'

He smiled and she shrank back as far as her seatbelt would allow. He had been impersonally friendly all day but his smile was little short of fiendish.

'Did you think,' he said, his voice pure acid, 'I would allow you free reign with my credit cards? You must think me a fool if you think I would trust you with a penny. It would be too good an opportunity to recover some of the money I deprived you of when I caught you with my wallet.'

Jan closed her eyes, desperately trying to shut out the sight of him, but his menacing smile and cold eyes were imprinted on her brain. Would he never believe her?

Their trip to London and their shared interest in the house brought an uneasy truce. They lived in harmony but only on the surface. Their relationship was like a woodland pool, Jan thought as she sat opposite Carlos on their last day in the flat. It was calm, even stagnant, on the surface, seemingly undisturbed by the smallest ripple, but underneath were hidden currents needing only the slightest breeze to bring them to life. This peaceful interlude wouldn't last; sooner or later Carlos would disclose his reason for the charade they were acting, and she had a strong suspicion she wouldn't like it at all.

Carlos looked up from the piece of toast he was eating and raised his eyebrows at the intense way Jan was gazing at him.

'Have I a smut on my nose, Jacinta? You are staring at me as if I have. Either that or you want me to make love to you.'

Jan blushed; she should be used to Carlos's provocative remarks by now, but they got to her every time.

'Neither, if you must know,' she said, ignoring the look in his eyes.

'Then you are wondering what will happen when we move into Over Grange. I think you do not need to wonder, do you?' he said enquiringly, grinning at the faint colour that stole into her face.

The move went smoothly, so smoothly Jan could hardly believe that only a few hours earlier they had been sharing breakfast in the flat surrounded by packing cases. Now they were in a small room that Jan, with Carlos's approval, had decided would serve as a dining-room when they were on their own. It was badly in need of decoration but it was tidy and, though she knew the cases were waiting to be unpacked, they could relax for the first time that day.

'This is my favourite meal of the day,' Jan said, biting into a small iced cake.

'I agree with you.' Carlos stretched his long legs out

and leaned back, only to sit upright, a pained expression on his face.

'*Diablo*! There is a spring in this chair that doesn't care for me.'

'Sorry, Carlos. I did warn you to treat it with respect. The new furniture for this room should be here next week.'

'I sincerely hope so,' Carlos grumbled, moving gingerly to the edge of his seat. 'Ring the suppliers up and tell them it is a matter of urgency they deliver on Monday.' He stretched out a hand and helped himself to a sandwich. 'These are very good. You have unsuspected talents, Jacinta. Later perhaps I shall look for a cook, or a married couple—the garden is too large for you to manage alone—but for now I look to you for the comfort I expect.'

His cold black eyes told her this was part of her punishment for daring to intrude in his life, and she bit her lip with small white teeth. She was very tired from the efforts she had put into making sure the move had been trouble-free and she wanted nothing more than to indulge in a hot bath and go straight to bed. She glanced at Carlos and, meeting his bland expression, knew she wouldn't be seeing her bed for hours. She would have to prepare dinner and he would expect a proper meal, not just a snack. She rubbed her finger over the delicate cup and sighed. 'Were you thinking of going out for dinner, Carlos? I don't think there is much food in the house.'

'On the contrary, Jacinta, there is everything we need for a meal. I knew you wouldn't have time for shopping so I did it for you while you were supervising the unloading.' He stood up. 'I shall have a stroll round the garden then a long, leisurely bath. I would like dinner promptly at seven.' He strode from the room; leaving

Jan feeling shattered.

Have a long, leisurely bath, would he, and a stroll round the garden, the rotten devil? He knew very well that was what she had been longing for for the last two hours. So much for his friendly mood of the last few days; Carlos was going to exact his revenge in every way he could. Well, she would do all he wanted, however hard it was. She would cook and clean till she was exhausted, but the one thing she wouldn't do was to sleep with him. His unyielding demands strengthened her resolve to find some way of proving her innocence, but now she had to cook a dinner he wouldn't sneer at.

After dinner they walked round the garden for a long time, engrossed in discovering the unusual bushes and trees the previous owner had planted and planning alterations Carlos wanted to make.

'You know far more than I do,' Jan said when for the third time he corrected her about the name for a shrub. 'You will have to teach me gardening.'

'I will be a very patient teacher,' Carlos said his voice deepening in a way that made Jan step hastily back. He pulled her to him, a strong arm whipping round her waist and his other hand holding her head still as she would have turned her face away.

'Don't fight me, Jacinta. I know you have taken a room as far from mine as you can get, but it won't do. Even if we didn't want each other you are my mistress and must sleep in the master suite with me. Why do you think I moved mountains to get it decorated and furnished by today?' His mouth came down on hers, crushing her lips with a force that combined anger and desire. Jan refused to open her mouth and he lifted his head and smiled before kissing her again, his tongue and lips caressing hers so gently that her lips opened to him involuntarily.

He murmured his satisfaction and took possession. Jan felt her mind reel under his onslaught; the seductive movement of his tongue against hers and the way his fingers touched her ears and throat made her head swim. She sighed and, putting her arms round his neck, ran her fingers through his thick crisp hair and down his neck and across his shoulders. She wanted to feel his skin without the barrier of his shirt and she tugged at it impatiently, finding without surprise that they were lying on a bed of soft grass and moss under sheltering trees.

She succeeded in undoing his shirt and Carlos groaned as she slid her fingers on to his skin. She caressed him feverishly, exploring his broad chest and shoulders, delighting in the feel of his velvet skin and pulling gently at the tangle of curls on his chest until he murmured.

'*Querida*, I want you. I can't wait any longer.' He pulled her bra undone and discarded it, throwing it on top of the jeans and shirt he had removed almost without her knowing. He seized her hand and placed it on the buckle of his belt.

'Undress me, Jacinta,' he said, his hands teasing her nipples erect. His dark eyes promised ecstasy but the touch of the cold metal brought her alive to what would happen if she didn't stop him right now. She twisted away, gasping with shock. How could she have let things go so far? Carlos's expression changed to anger and his hands on her shoulders bit into her flesh.

'Do not play games, Jacinta, or do you want a fight?' His eyes darkened. 'Is that what you want?'

'No, Carlos, no. Let me go. I don't want—I don't——'

His face hardened and he sat up, his mouth curled in contempt.

'So you were teasing, trying out your power. You bitch! You are determined I shall make love to you against all my instincts, to have me grovel for your favours.' He shook her sharply. 'Is that what you want, Jacinta? It won't happen. I want you, but there are many women who will come at a click of my fingers. I have no need for soiled goods and you are soiled, Jacinta, both by your criminal activities and your former lovers.' His eyes raked over her and Jan quivered at the arrogant way his gaze roamed over every inch of her body.

She scrambled to her feet and threw her clothes on without looking in his direction. His hands flexed at his sides and she touched one pleadingly.

'Please, Carlos, I didn't mean to tease.' Her soft words had an effect and Jan sighed with relief as his whole form relaxed and he picked up his shirt.

'I will suspend your punishment,' he said slowly and Jan knew it was a concession to himself and not to her. He looked at her out of eyes that were dark and as blank as outer space must be, and, taking her arm, walked with her back to the house.

Jan ran water into the sink and started to wash up, hoping Carlos would offer to help her. It had been a long day and she wanted to go to bed and sleep and sleep. Carlos looked past her at the piles of dishes. Jan was a fair cook but she had managed to use every knife, fork, spoon and bowl the kitchen boasted.

'You could do with some help,' he drawled. 'Pity the dishwasher isn't connected, but it will stop you having time on your hands, won't it?' He smiled sardonically

and returned to his study. Jan kicked the unoffending
dishwasher. If she knew Carlos he had made sure it
wouldn't work until it suited him. She flung her head
back. She wouldn't give him the satisfaction of knowing
his little tricks upset her, and she set about her task with
renewed vigour.

When the kitchen was as neat and clean as it could be
she went to her room, a triumphant smile curving her
lips. She had no intention of moving from the small
room she had selected for herself. Carlos had been very
insistent that they should share a room, but she couldn't
see why it was so important. This room was as far away
as it could be from the master suite but it was still too
near for comfort. She undressed quickly, pulling on a
flimsy nightdress. It was a good thing no one would see
her in it. It drifted round her softly, the pale pink silk
revealing more than it concealed. She turned out the
bedside lamp and lay trying not to think of Carlos.

It was impossible. She could feel his presence through
the thick walls and floors that separated them as if he
were in the same room. She flung an arm over her head,
her fingers playing with a lock of hair. What was it about
Carlos that made her aware of him to the exclusion of
every other man she had ever known? She tensed and
shook her head. She loved Wade; how could she put
Carlos in front of him, even for a moment? She sighed
and turned her head away from the window through
which the moonlight streamed, filling the room with a
silvery light that touched everything with an unreal
enchantment.

As unreal and as distant as Wade and their love for
each other seemed.

The phone call she had made to Spain had left a host
of unanswered questions. Subconsciously doubts had

crept into her mind. Wade had been very plausible, too plausible, and her confidence in him had faltered. She sat up, clasping her hands round her knees.

The last thing she should do was doubt Wade and the first thing she should do was clear her name, but how? If she could speak to Wade again . . . She leaned against her pillows and clasped her hands behind her head, a smile on her lips. Not Wade, he knew nothing, but what of the other men who had been in Spain with him? She could only remember the name of one of them, David Long. She had met him once and had wondered at the close friendship that seemed to exist between him and Wade, as they seemed to have nothing in common. Was it possible that he or the other man was involved with the theft? Perhaps Wade was suspicious of one of them and feared that to come to her defence would put that man in jeopardy. She unclasped her hands, letting her arms fall to her sides. It was such a tangle of right and wrong and divided loyalties, but one thing was becoming clear: Wade's love for her was non-existent.

Her love for him was equally suspect—or was she just passing through a phase she would be ashamed of when this mess was finally cleared up and she and Wade could resume their relationship as it had been before she was accused of theft? She groaned and knew that could never happen. Carlos had come between them and her feelings for him were completely different from the way she thought of Wade.

It would be so easy to do as he wished and become his mistress, but without even thinking much about it she knew she wanted to go to her bridegroom a virgin. It wasn't the fashion, girls seemed almost to queue up to join the permissive society, but there must be some who thought differently. She smiled wryly. If Carlos had his way she would soon join the majority, but Carlos wasn't going to have his way. Jan shook her head emphatically at the thought and nestling down amongst her pillows closed her eyes.

The door opened with a crash and the light, turned on by an impatient hand, banished the gentle moonlight. Jan shot up in bed as Carlos stormed into the room and whipped the bed clothes away, despite her efforts to hold on to them.

'I thought I told you not to sleep in this room,' he said in a deceptively soft voice and Jan shivered at the menace under the tight control.

'I didn't think you were serious,' she said faintly.

'You know I was. You just chose to ignore me and I don't like being ignored. I have just completed two hours' solid work and I expected you to be waiting for me. A cold, empty bed isn't my idea of a loving woman.'

'I won't sleep with you, Carlos. I—will—not.' Jan spaced the last words out, emphasising them as if he might not understand unless she spoke very clearly. An amused gleam in the dark eyes that roamed over her body as she sat huddled against the pillows, her legs drawn up and her arms wrapped round her, informed her he understood not only her words but the difficulty she was having in rejecting him. He knew how hard she was having to fight her own longings to be in his arms, and his expression said he was amused by her reluctance.

He scooped her from the bed as if she weighed no more than a moonbeam and strode out of the room.

'Don't scream, *querida*. There is no one to hear you if you do. We are alone in the house, remember?' Jan did remember. She leaned limply against him and gave herself up to the joy of being in his arms. All too soon he reached the master suite and lowered her to the ground.

He closed the door and pocketed the key but Jan had no wish to escape. She admired afresh the lovely room, its scheme of apricot, cream and jade-green a lovely compliment to her own colouring.

'You can bring your clothes here tomorrow, and to make sure you do I will help you.' He walked across the deep cream carpet and opened the door leading to his room. 'I think you had forgotten there are two bedrooms,' he said, with a twist of his lips. 'I have no intention of raping you, Jacinta. I only want you as my mistress in the sight of the world; I cannot yet bring myself to follow in the wake of your other lovers.'

Jan opened her mouth to shout that she had no other lovers but a look at his dark, brooding face made her close her lips firmly. For all his denials, she was in danger. Carlos, like the proverbial lady, was protesting far too much. He might despise her as a thief, but the flame in his eyes told her it wouldn't take much to make him forget both his wallet and the formula. If he thought she had other lovers it might act as another barrier.

He closed the door, cutting off Jan's view of the room that was decorated in deeper, richer tones of the same colours as her own. She took a deep breath, splashed her face with cold water in the bathroom that echoed her bedroom and got into the wide bed. She had thought it would be impossible to be so near to Carlos and sleep, but she only awoke as the sun's rays traced a shining path across her eyelids after a dreamless, refreshing night.

'I have to go to the pottery this morning,' Carlos said as Jan placed a plate of bacon, eggs, mushrooms and tomatoes before him. 'I shan't be back for lunch so, as you will have time on your hands, make sure dinner is special.' He signed to Jan to pour his coffee and she longed to throw the pot at him. During the last week Jan had wilted under the burden of work Carlos had thrust on to her slim shoulders. He expected her to clean the house and provide meals of a very high standard, criticising any dish that didn't meet his approval, and more than once she had wanted to throw it at him, resisting the urge only because of the look in his eyes that promised swift retribution.

In addition to acting as his housekeeper and cook, she carried the whole burden of getting the house decorated and furnished to Carlos's liking. She had consulted him from time to time, only to be told that the responsibility was hers and that he would let her know if she did anything he disliked, sending a quiver of fear through Jan's nerves at the thought of his anger if she did make a mistake. But as the days passed and he had seemed to approve her choice of colours and materials, Jan had relaxed, telling herself it was just a job she must carry out to the best of her ability.

She looked up from her musings to find his eyes fixed on her. 'I hope you are planning a meal for tonight and not wondering if you can empty the coffee over my head and get away with it.'

Jan gasped; he was doing it again. 'Stop reading my mind,' she snapped, putting the pot down and gasping as she realised what she had said.

'It is written all over your very expressive face but, I warn you, punishment would land just as swiftly on your head.' He smiled and returned to his breakfast.

As soon as Jan heard his car roar down the drive on its way to the pottery she walked quickly to the study and, sitting down at the old table that did duty for a desk, drew the telephone towards her. She had decided to try to contact David Long. Perhaps he might know something that would help her. Her fingers closed tightly round the receiver. She didn't even know if David Long was still in England, and, if he was, he wouldn't be likely to say anything against Wade.

Ten minutes later she left the study, a smile on her pale face. David Long had been puzzled by her request for a meeting, but reluctantly he had given in to her urgings and they had arranged to meet at lunch time in a small park a few miles from the pottery. Her mind very much on the coming meeting, Jan nevertheless remembered Carlos's demands for a special dinner. She looked at the only cookery book she had and made a list of food she must buy after she had seen Wade's friend.

Wade. She pushed the list into her bag, wishing she could as easily push away the unhappiness the thought of Wade brought. She could no longer delude herself; he had used her to deflect suspicion from whoever had removed the formula from room three. She closed her eyes in anguish. Wade had been her first love; she had thought they would marry and live together all the rest of their lives, and if Wade hadn't taken the wrong path they would have done just that.

She dressed in a dark brown cotton dress with an orange belt and, leaving the matching orange jacket behind her as too conspicuous, caught a bus to the park. Carlos had hinted about a car for her use but his mocking tone and the failure of the car to appear made it one more thing to taunt her with. Mistresses might merit cars, thieves don't, his tone had said very clearly.

The small park was an oasis of green with heavy old Victorian-looking benches set among bushes. Jan sat down in a clearing that held a solitary seat near a pond. She had barely settled when a man stepped from between two large shrubs.

CHAPTER SIX

JAN looked at David Long curiously; their one meeting had been very brief. She knew he was an accountant but that was all. He was shorter than Wade and heavily built with brown hair already showing signs of grey at the temples. He was about the same age as Carlos, but Carlos's air of command and distinction was replaced, in this man, by a look of bitter intolerance with the world and everyone in it.

Jan's heart sank. She doubted if she would get any help from this man. It had been a mistake to meet him, but she had to try to find a way out of the pit she had fallen into and perhaps she was wrong about him. She smiled. His eyes flickered slightly and Jan held out her hand.

'Hello, David,' she said, moving slightly, inviting him to sit down. After a moment he did, ignoring her hand and sprawling on the bench as far away from her as he could.

'What do you want to see me about?' he said, his harsh voice grating on her tender nerves.

Jan looked at him but he was gazing into the pond, apparently absorbed with a leaf that was drifting lazily to and fro, propelled by an errant breeze. Straight and to the point, Jan thought wryly. Well, that suited her, she didn't want to be alone with him for longer than necessary; there was something about him that chilled her blood.

'I'm sure Wade has told you something of the trouble I am in,' she said quietly.

'Something. You stole a formula, didn't you? Now that was very silly of you, but I don't see what it has to do with me.'

'I haven't stolen anything,' Jan said indignantly. 'You were with Wade at the time the formula was taken and ...'

'You think one of us had something to do with it?' He turned to her, his hard brown eyes boring into hers. 'That's not a nice thing to think about your fiancé and his friend, now, is it?' His voice was soft but Jan didn't believe he was saying what he really wanted to say. She stroked the leather of her bag, taking pleasure in touching something familiar. She looked into eyes that reminded her of a snake and tried to smile; it wouldn't achieve anything to antagonise him.

'No, it's not nice, and I didn't mean that I think either you or Wade are involved—how could I? You were in Spain—but I do think you might know who is responsible.'

'You think I would betray that someone?'

Jan sighed. She had imagined the look in his eyes when she had mentioned Spain; it seemed ludicrous now that she had thought David Long could and would help her. She crossed her ankles and answered him.

'No, I don't suppose you would betray anyone, but as you have pointed out I am engaged to Wade and deserve his loyalty.'

'But not mine. I suggest you ask Wade the questions you have asked me. If I knew the answers, if I did, it wouldn't pay me to tell you. Men who steal things worth nearly a million pounds play rough if anyone talks out of turn.' He got up and, ignoring Jan's gasp at the amount of money the formula was worth, stood over her.

'I have one piece of advice for you, and that is to keep

your mouth shut before someone shuts it for you.' He disappeared as quickly as he had come and Jan sat very still, waiting for the lingering menace to leave her. She wished she had never met David Long; she sensed an evil in him that made her shudder. How could Wade have anything to do with such a man, let alone claim him as his friend?

She got up and walked quickly away from the little pond that all at once seemed dark and sinister. Wade couldn't know what David Long was really like or he would see that David was using him as Wade had, in his turn, used her.

She shopped for food, not really knowing what it was she bought, and returned to Over Grange as soon as she could, the heavy baskets making her arms ache long before she reached the house. A sense of homecoming made her sigh with relief as she opened the door. Carlos made her work hard but he also protected her from such people as David Long. She sat at the kitchen table and thought about her meeting. It had been a lost hope from the first. David was right; she must talk to Wade, now.

The receptionist in Spain connected her with Wade with the minimum of fuss, and tension drained from Jan as she heard his voice.

'Jan?' he said and she laughed at the surprise dancing down the wires. What an idiot she had been. Wade was her love and all would be well.

'Jan,' he said again and this time she answered him, and leaving nothing out, told him about her meeting with David Long.

'He said I should ask you anything I wanted to know and he was right; I shouldn't have involved him.'

'No, Jan, you shouldn't and his advice to you is good. It's best not to say anything to anyone, particularly del

Raimondes.' His voice softened. 'You're making an unholy fuss about nothing. I've cleared things with del Raimondes, as I told you before. What more can I do?'

'I don't know,' Jan said sadly. 'He still thinks I'm guilty.'

'That's too bad,' he said and Jan gripped the receiver with fingers that were suddenly icy. Wade would have been more concerned if she had cut her finger.

'Remember what David advised,' he said sharply when she didn't speak. 'Just do your work and keep quiet. I'll be in touch. Bye for now, Jan.' He replaced the receiver and she listened to the dialling tone for several seconds before putting the phone down.

She laid her head on the old table and cried, the tears running down her face, until she could cry no more. Wade hadn't even remembered she was suspended from the pottery. She was certain now that he was mixed up in the theft of the formula. Had he planned to use her to cover up for the real culprit all along? Had he ever loved her? She wanted to give him the benefit of the doubt, wanted to believe that, for a time at least, Wade had loved her as much as she had loved him. Her sore heart made the tears flow again but she dashed them away with an angry hand. She wasn't the first girl to be taken in by a smooth talker and she would get over it, but why did Wade have to throw her to Carlos? Surely his own sense would have told him Carlos wasn't the kind of man who would take the loss of something he had spent years on without fighting back. Or had he counted on Carlos, satisfied that he had caught his thief, ceasing to look in any other direction? If so, he had been right, and the fact of the formula being the wrong one hadn't made any difference. Someone had violated his trust, stolen his property, and he intended to have his revenge.

She got to her feet, casting a startled glance at the clock; Carlos would be home in less than two hours and she had dinner to cook. She didn't know how she managed it but somehow she did sufficiently well to bring a smile to Carlos's lips.

'You are turning out to be a very good cook, Jacinta,' he said as they sat in the drawing-room after dinner.

'I'm glad you're pleased,' Jan said wearily. Every bone in her body seemed to ache. She had been up at six and she had been on the move all day, cleaning, cooking and making sure the decorators carried out her orders correctly, in addition to her abortive attempt to clear her name. She couldn't blame Carlos for being so savage about the theft, not when a million pounds were involved.

Carlos's exclamation and the splash of his brandy on to the table made her aware that she had uttered her last thought out loud. She stared at him in horror as he pulled her out of her chair and thrust her on to the settee, twisting her round to face him.

'So,' he purred, 'at last we come to the truth. You expected to get one million for my formula?' Jan tried to disregard his painful grip on her arms and met the burning rage in his eyes as bravely as she could.

'I haven't tried to sell your formula, Carlos. I have never had it to sell. I was thinking about something I heard today and unfortunately repeated it aloud.' His grip tightened until Jan only just prevented herself from crying out.

'Where did you hear this interesting snippet, Jacinta?'

Jan groaned inwardly. Any hope of keeping her meeting with David Long and the phone call to Wade secret was fading fast. She looked up at the hard black eyes set in a grim face, much too near for comfort, and sighed.

'I will tell you if you will stop trying to crush my poor bones to powder,' she said with a little gasp of pain. Carlos let his hands fall from her arms and Jan rubbed the tender flesh gingerly; she would have bruises by the morning. Carlos's dark eyes showed not the slightest glimmer of repentance.

'Start your story, Jacinta. I am eager to know how you will explain knowledge only the thief could have.'

Jan pushed her hair back from her face and quietly told him all that had passed between her and David Long. After she had finished speaking Carlos sat for several minutes, his face a mask and his eyes blank. At last, just as Jan reached screaming point, he moved.

'Interesting. I wonder where David Long got that figure from.'

'Then it's the right one?'

'Give or take a few thousands, yes, it's correct.'

'Then you know I have told you the truth,' Jan breathed, hardly able to believe that at last Carlos could no longer think she was a thief.

'I believe you have told the truth about your meeting with Long, but there is more to come.'

She might have known she couldn't keep anything from him. Jan nodded and related her phone call to Spain, the memory of how indifferent Wade had been to her troubles bringing tears to her eyes. Carlos seized her left hand, making Jan aware that she had been touching her ring finger, a habit she had formed since Wade had asked her to marry him in what seemed another life.

'What is Wade Felton to you?' he asked harshly. Jan parted her lips to say they were finished but, remembering that however much Carlos despised both her and himself, he wanted her, she changed her mind.

'We are engaged,' she said calmly. Carlos's breath escaped in a ragged hiss and his hand tightened on hers. She would be black and blue if he continued like that, Jan thought.

'You aren't wearing his ring.'

'Wade is bringing it back from Spain next time he comes.'

'How will he take the knowledge that you are my mistress?'

Jan looked at him blankly. That aspect of the case had completely escaped her. If Wade loved her ... But he didn't, so he wouldn't care.

'He will understand when I tell him why I am posing as your mistress. He does know you thought I was a thief, but he also thinks he has set things right.'

'Oh, he does? I still think you stole both my wallet and the glaze. Your story was brilliant but just too pat, designed to make me think you innocent and that I have treated you badly.' His eyes narrowed. 'That's it, isn't it, Jacinta? My remorse would blind me to your future activities.'

'What activities? I don't understand.'

'Oh, I think you do. The real formula is still in my possession; I would be the fool you take me for if I didn't know it is still in danger.'

Jan dropped her eyes from his; it was she who was the fool. David Long had intended her to let slip her knowledge about the money, he had thought Carlos would fall for her story. But what would be the advantage to David in that? Don't forget Wade, her tired brain reminded her, he's in as deep as David.

Carlos rose and towered over her.

'You and Felton are a good pair,' he grated. 'Your

pathetic story has failed to convince me of your innocence but it has achieved one thing. I no longer desire you in my bed tonight as I had intended before your fairytale.' He turned away, speaking over his shoulder. 'You have a reprieve, but only a reprieve. Your engagement means nothing to me; we shall be lovers soon.'

Jan came down to breakfast on Tuesday morning in a more settled state of mind. Nothing had really changed between herself and Carlos, her position was still that of supposed mistress, but at least he was no longer pressing her to make the title a reality, and she hoped that in time they could be friendly and dispense with play-acting. More than that she dared not hope for.

Carlos, seated at a small table in the gloomy dining-room, looked up from his letters and glared at her. Jan's heart sank. What had brought that on? She smiled and wished him a bright good morning but he only grunted.

'How much longer do we have to eat in this dungeon?' he said. 'What has happened to your plans for the small dining-room?'

'It should be ready by the end of the week,' Jan said quietly.

'What about the drawing-room, my study and the rest of the bedrooms?' he snapped.

'The drawing-room also at the end of the week. Your study will be another two days, but the bedrooms aren't due to be started until the rooms I have mentioned are finished.'

'When will this room be ready?'

A startled look crept into Jan's eyes. 'I thought we had agreed that this room could wait until the rest of the house is finished.'

'How long will that be? I am tired of living in a badly

furnished barn. I want you to put this room in hand and
two of the bedrooms must be ready by the beginning of
next week. It shouldn't be too difficult if you put your
back into it,' he sneered. 'It is also time you did some
work on your designs; I want the series ready for the
potters as soon as possible. You may have to put in some
overtime but I am paying you handsomely when I would
be justified in taking your paintings in part payment for
your crime.'

Jan pushed her half-eaten bacon and eggs to one side
and leaned towards him, her eyes huge violet pools in her
pale face.

'Is it any use my asking you to believe that I am not
the person you want? I didn't and don't know anything
about it. I am not an expert on glazes; I don't know how
different yours is from any other. As far as I am aware it
might not be any good.'

Carlos's eyes darkened. 'So that is your line, Jacinta. It
does not convince me of your innocence.' He picked up
his coffee. 'The subject is closed. I am more interested in
the state of this house.'

'Is there any special reason for such urgency?' Jan
said bitterly. No matter what she said, Carlos was
determined to think she was guilty.

He reached for a piece of toast and spread marmalade
sparingly before he answered.

'We are having guests, as I thought we might. Eat
your breakfast, Jacinta, they are not coming today.'

'When are they arriving?'

Carlos flicked a finger at the letter beside his plate. 'A
week today, so you have seven days to get this place in
order. Don't fail me, Jacinta.'

'How many visitors, Carlos, and are they important?'

'Two, both female and as for important, they could

be.'

Jan caught her breath, a flash of intuition striking her.

'That's what this is all about, isn't it, Carlos? Our pretence?' She waved her hand round the room. 'This whole set up is for their benefit, isn't it. Who are they, Carlos?'

'You have a right to know, indeed you must know, and yes, my uninvited guests are partly the reason we are both here.' He pushed his cup aside. 'We will go into the study, it is comfortable if shabby, and I will tell you what you want to know.'

'Or as much as you think I should know.'

'How well you know me, Jacinta; too well. I am not sure I like your perception when I am the target.'

That followed. He was a very private person; he had gone to a great deal of trouble and expense to set the stage for these unknown visitors and only now, because it was important she didn't make mistakes, was he about to tell her the reason. She sat down in a worn leather armchair that was surprisingly comfortable and wondered if it would be a good idea to have it re-upholstered. Her attention drifted to the carpet—that would have to go—and on to possible colour schemes.

'Not blue or too much black,' Carlos said firmly and she jumped; he had read her mind once again.

'You were going to tell me about your visitors,' Jan said, her eyes on the floor. She was determined she wouldn't say anything about his uncomfortable habit of knowing what she was thinking almost before she did herself.

'Ah yes, my guests. There is my mother and her goddaughter.' He crossed one long, immaculately clad leg over the other. 'For a long time my mother and more particularly my grandfather have been urging me to marry. Most Spaniards are married long before they are thirty-five and I shall reach that age in a few months. My grandfather wants an heir. He completely disregards my three cousins as they are not of the direct line and insists I marry and provide him with grandchildren. I have no intention of marrying, either now or in the future, but he is old and grows increasingly impatient. Hence my visitors.'

'I take it,' Jan said slowly, her brows puckered, 'that the second of your visitors is an eligible young woman?'

'She is. For years I have been introduced to all the daughters of Spain, or so it seems. Alva Costos is the granddaughter of an old friend of my grandfather. Our families have always been close and therefore I have to be on my guard. That is why you are here, Jacinta. A mistress in residence should be a good deterrent.'

'You make me sound like an insect spray,' Jan said. 'I had worked it out for myself but I still don't like it. It will be very embarrassing and quite unnecessary. You have only to refrain from proposing. However modern Miss Costos is, I am sure she won't ask you to marry her.'

'No, but I wouldn't put it past my mother to contrive to compromise the girl in such a way that in her and my grandfather's eyes I would have no choice but to marry her.'

'I can't see you doing that, however damning the conditions were,' Jan said, dismay at the thought of Carlos asking the Spanish girl to marry him curling through her.

'I certainly would not, but it could cause trouble and I want to avoid that.'

'You think having me here will prevent an upset?' Jan asked in amazement. 'It is far more likely to cause it.'

'You can leave that kind of trouble to me. My mother

is a woman of the world; she will know an accomplished fact when she sees one.'

A week of hard work sped by and Jan hoped Carlos was right. All his plans would go for nothing if Señora del Raimondes decided that Jan wasn't an obstacle to the marriage of Carlos and her goddaughter. Early in the week Carlos had engaged the married couple he had said he would. He had contacted a top agency and decided that Mr and Mrs Kent, the fourth couple he had interviewed, would be very satisfactory, so Jan was relieved of the cleaning and cooking. However, her days had still been long and tiring. In additon to supervising the decorators she had hung curtains, pushed furniture into place and added all the special touches that make a house into a home.

She had also worked at her designs, getting up early to spend time she should have spent sleeping in making sure Carlos would have nothing to complain of where her real work was concerned, and when it seemed as if even that wouldn't give her time enough she had crept into the room she used as an office after Carlos had retired for the night.

Until last night, when a furious Carlos confronted her as she drooped at her desk, too tired to go to bed.

'I didn't ask you to kill yourself, Jacinta,' he said angrily. 'You cannot pay for your crime if you are ill.' He pulled her from her chair, slung her over his shoulder and deposited her on her bed. Jan struggled up and faced him, her head high.

'I have only been doing as you ordered,' she stormed. 'The designs you want are finished.'

'Am I supposed to cheer? I didn't state a time, but I am glad you are conscious of your debt. When my visitors have arrived you can design a second set of plates with foreign butterflies and plants.' Jan seized a pillow from the bed and threw it, but he stepped smartly to one side and behind the door of his room.

To her surprise, Carlos returned to her room with a large parcel which he handed to Jan, instructing her to unpack it carefully.

'If you break anything, Jacinta, you will pay for it,' he drawled with a sardonic look that said it wouldn't be money with which she paid. She unpacked it carefully, crying out in delight when she discovered the china figures she had admired when they had shopped for the carpets and curtains.

'Oh, how gorgeous! They will be just right in the alcove in the drawing-room.' Impulsively she flung her arms round his neck and kissed him on his mouth. Carlos pulled her close to him, his eyes hard and enigmatic.

'So that's what it takes for you to kiss me,' he murmured. 'I must bring presents more often.' He put her away from him with a restrained power that was more anger than love.

'But don't make the mistake,' he said smoothly, 'of thinking these figures are just for you. I, too, think they will look good in the drawing-room.' He carried the box from the bedroom and Jan followed him, blinking tears from her lashes. She had made the mistake of thinking he had bought the china because she had fallen in love with it, and she had paid the price, receiving his contempt and cynicism once again.

Jan moved a copper jug filled with white delphiniums an inch to the left, then moved it back into its original position. She stood with her head on one side and admired its shining beauty against the dark oak of the hall. There were other urns of flowers and leaves standing on the wide, polished oak floorboards that reflected the elegant curve of the staircase, the walls of which were still waiting for the paintings they needed.

She drifted into the drawing-room. She had been guided here by the magnificent painted ceiling, and had picked up the jade-green and white of the oval medallions, where cupids sported among clusters of roses, in the carpet and curtains. She had added a deeper shade of green and the delicate pink of the painted roses in the upholstery of the comfortable chairs and settees. It still needed more ornaments; the figures Carlos had bought in London looked lovely in the white painted alcove, but the room was so large it wanted something bigger.

She checked her appearance in the beautiful old Venetian mirror over the fireplace and tucked a loose strand of hair back into place with nervous fingers. Her dress was simple, pale pink and sleeveless, very suitable both for the time of day and for meeting unknown guests, but it wasn't in the least sophisticated and she wondered if Carlos would want her to change. She wished he would come out of his study; he had been in there all day and he must know his visitors were due.

A car drawing up and Carlos's appearance coincided. He put his arm round her and kissed her as the doorbell rang.

'Play up to me, Jacinta. Don't forget we are in love and living together.' He kissed her again, bringing colour to her sensitive skin. 'Keep that up and we have won,' he said, a mischievous glint in his eyes. Jan laughed, but she was glad of his hand holding hers as the young girl she had engaged during the week opened the door.

The woman who entered was tall, dark-haired and

elegant, but otherwise not in the least like her son.

'Carlos!' She smiled and kissed him delicately on his cheek. She held him away from her, her words coming quickly in a flood of Spanish. She turned and drew her companion forward. Jan didn't have to hear the name Alva to know this was the girl Carlos was expected to marry. With a sinking heart she saw that the other girl was beautiful, with a perfection of features not often seen in real life. Her olive skin was faultless and her raven hair, swathed round her head, was thick and glossy, and she was tall, standing at least five feet ten inches in her high-heeled shoes. She wore a dark red silk suit with an assured ease that made Jan feel small and insignificant.

Alva put her arms round Carlos's neck and kissed him full on his mouth. He returned it with more interest than Jan thought he should have shown, before disengaging her arms and, stretching out a hand, bringing Jan to his side.

'Jacinta, this is my mother and her goddaughter, Alva Costos. Mother, Alva, this is Jacinta Shelley, who is the mistress of my house.'

Much as she deplored the whole thing Jan secretly admired Carlos for the way he had made her position clear without actually putting it into words. His mother's eyes widened and she looked at Jan with a puzzled stare. She covered her feelings quickly and murmured something in Spanish, ignoring the hand Jan held out. She let it fall to her side, catching Carlos's furious glare as his mother turned away on pretence of taking off her coat. The Spanish girl held out a limp hand and murmured something in Spanish and Jan saw Carlos smile warmly at her.

'Tea is ready. Won't you come into the drawing-room?' Jan asked, hoping to smooth over an awkward moment. Señora del Raimondes walked past her saying something in Spanish over her shoulder to Carlos.

'Speak English, Mother. Jan doesn't know much Spanish yet.'

'I am not surprised. The English have no gift for languages other than their own barbaric one. Even the well educated fail in this,' his mother said, leaving no shadow of doubt that she didn't consider Jan to have any education at all. 'It is a good thing Alva has received a good education, my son, one suitable for the wife of an important man.'

'Is Señorita Costos hoping to be married?' Jan asked, her innocence as phoney as the *señora's* politeness.

'All Spanish girls of good family hope to be married, and in the *señorita's* case I am convinced it will not be long before she is.'

Alva smiled complacently, her dark eyes looking confidently at Carlos, and Jan wished she could empty the teapot over her head.

'No, Jacinta,' Carlos said quietly but clearly, a spark of amusement in his eyes. 'Pour the tea in the cups please, *querida*.'

Alva looked puzzled but accepted the cup Jan handed her. She sipped the tea with an expression of distaste but bravely drank half a cup. The *señora* didn't even lift the cup from its saucer.

'I do not like tea, Carlos, as you know very well. I will take coffee.'

'I am sorry, *señora*, I will ask Mrs Kent to make you some.' Jan put down the teapot, but Carlos stopped her with a wave of his hand.

'This is England, Mother, and in my house we drink tea in the afternoon.'

Jan looked at him in dismay. He was doing his best to

upset his mother and, by the look on her face, he was succeeding.

Jan stood before her wardrobe looking at her clothes; there were far more of them than she had possessed in the whole of her life. She put out a hand and took a pale yellow chiffon dinner dress off its hanger. She couldn't stand here for ever; the evening had to be faced and with it dinner in company with Carlos's mother and Alva. Jan put her dress on her bed and, sitting in front of the dressing-table, started to brush her hair. There was something soothing in the smooth, regular strokes, and a little of the tension that had been building up ever since Carlos's visitors had arrived gradually left her.

The tea party, if you could call it that, had gone from bad to dreadful. The *señora*, making no pretence of drinking tea or of eating the dainty cakes Mrs Kent had provided, demanded to see her room. She made for the door, summoning Jan with a flick of her fingers as if she were a servant, and Carlos looked as if he were about to explode. Jan put a hand on his arm, gave him a brief smile and followed his mother. Alva lingered, murmuring something in Spanish that brought a smile to Carlos's grim features, and Jan saw a satisfied expression on his mother's face before she called to her goddaughter.

'Come, Alva, we must find our rooms, you will have plenty of time to talk to Carlos later this evening.'

Alva stretched up to her full height and kissed Carlos on his cheek and Jan felt a pang of pure hatred as Carlos laughed and in his turn pressed his lips to the girl's smooth skin.

The *señora* had protested strongly about the rooms she and Alva had been given. They were too small, altogether too insignificant; Alva especially should have a room reflecting her future prestige. The *señora* looked slyly at Jan as, with a smile that was supposed to be sincere, she said they could hope for interesting events between Carlos and Alva in the near future.

'You will then desire to find other employment and it is possible I can help you. I have friends with establishments of importance; one of them, I am sure, will be able to employ a house mistress of your abilities.' She smiled at Jan as if she had solved all their problems.

It slowly dawned on Jan that the *señora*, understanding English imperfectly, had misunderstood Carlos when he had said she was the mistress of his house. She suppressed a chuckle; so much for Carlos and his adroit way of telling his mother that Jan was his mistress. He had only convinced her that she was his housekeeper.

'I am sorry, *señora*,' Jan said, struggling not to laugh. 'These are the only rooms available. None of the others have been decorated yet.'

'This I do not believe,' the *señora* said and pushing past Jan swept out of the room with an arrogance worthy of her son. She opened the door of the next room and turned angrily to Jan.

'This room is freshly painted,' she accused.

'Yes, it is the room I thought the *señorita* could have.'

'Too small, and the cupboard for clothes is hopeless,' Alva said, peering over Jan's shoulder at the pretty room as if it were little better than a dog kennel. Alva opened the next door and frowned as she saw it was stripped ready for the painters.

'All the other rooms are the same size,' Jan said trying to keep pace with her as she opened door after door.

'There must be some rooms in order,' she said. She darted away and opened Jan's door.

'Oh, yes, I knew there would be one.' She turned reproachful eyes to Jan. 'This room is entirely suitable, why have you not shown this room before? I do not like the colours, too pale, but there is a big place for clothes.' She flung open the wardrobe revealing a rich and colourful array of clothes.

'This is my room,' Jan said quietly.

'Your room?' Danger signals flashed in both pairs of dark eyes and Jan stood her ground with an effort. She nodded, and the *señora* wrenched angrily at the nearest dresses, almost tearing them from the hangers and throwing them at Jan until she was practically smothered under the folds of silks and velvets.

'This is not the right room for you,' Alva said icily. 'How could you put Carlos's *madre* in a servant's room while you sleep here?' She opened the chest of drawers. 'How do you have such fine clothes?' She held up a nightdress of finely embroidered silk and lace. 'This is for a bride, not for a person who keeps house.' She didn't wait for an answer but continued to examine the contents of the drawer while the *señora* did the same with the wardrobe. Jan sank on to the bed and listened to the two women commenting on her clothes with complete detachment.

Where, she wondered vaguely, was Carlos? His fine plans were falling about his ears. She should be pleased, but she only felt cold as if something terrible was about to overtake her.

'I shall occupy this chamber,' Alva said and Jan felt strongly that she didn't want Alva to sleep in her room next to Carlos. She was a very beautiful woman and both she and the *señora* were determined Alva should marry Carlos, but Jan was just as determined that she shouldn't. Without questioning why the thought of Carlos and Alva joined in matrimony should be so painful, she knew she would do anything in her power to prevent such a thing happening.

'Is this another bedroom?' the *señora* asked, pointing to the connecting door to Carlos's room. 'Well, Miss Shelley, answer me?'

Jan nodded, unable to speak if it had meant her life. She could only sit and wait for what she sensed would happen. The *señora* stretched out her hand to the door as it opened, and Carlos appeared, stopping short at the scene before his eyes. He was wearing dark trousers and a white shirt unbuttoned to the waist and the colour rose in the Spanish girl's face at the sight of his broad chest with its line of dark hair that disappeared under his waistband.

'*Dios*! What is going on? What are you doing with Jacinta's clothes?' he said, unhurriedly doing up his shirt.

'Jacinta, please explain why my mother and Alva are in your room sorting through your clothes as if they were at a sale? Put that down,' he roared at Alva as she held a sea-green nightdress against herself. 'It does not suit you and it belongs to Jacinta.' Alva cast the nightdress on one side and ran to him, pressing against him.

'I do not know what is this sale, and you are right, Carlos, the garment is not my colour.'

Carlos shook her hand from his arm, strode over to Jan, plucked her from the bed and shook her.

'Come out of the dream you are in, Jacinta, and tell me what is going on.'

Jan blinked and Carlos came into focus along with the indignant figure of his mother. She smiled gently at the angry man who was gripping her arm tightly.

'Your mother thinks I am your housekeeper,' she said, enjoying the range of expressions that followed one another across Carlos's face.

'Housekeeper? Oh!'

'Yes, Oh. You were a bit too clever; your mother doesn't understand English as well as you do.' A giggle escaped her, stifled at once by the gleam in his eyes.

'I shall make myself clear,' he said and, turning to his mother, his arm round Jan's shoulders, he proceeded to leave them in no doubt as to the place Jan occupied both in his house and his life.

'This woman is your, your ...' the *señora* choked, leaving her sentence unfinished.

'Mistress is the word you require, Mother. She is, and you will give her the respect due to the mistress of my home,' he said, a note of warning in his voice.

'I cannot and will not give any respect to such a woman.' Jan flinched at the contempt in her tone. 'You should be ashamed, my son, to expect your mother and an innocent girl like Alva to live in the same house as a low woman.'

'*Silencio*!' Carlos roared. 'I do not expect you to live here. You are my guests and as my mother you are welcome, but this is Jacinta's home. She is the mistress here in all ways and you will show her the respect due to her.' He turned to Alva, making her squeal at his sudden movement. 'I suggest you replace those clothes where you found them. I am sure my mother will help you.' He tightened his grip on Jan's arm and they were out of the room in seconds, leaving behind them two people who had had all their ideas turned upside down.

Jan put her brush down and coiled her hair on top of her head. She dreaded the idea of facing the *señora* and Alva at dinner and wished she had the courage to stay in her room, but that would mean a scene with Carlos, though he must know that his idea of using her as a barrier to his mother's plans wasn't going to work. Jan had seen the determination showing through the shock Carlos had given his mother. She wouldn't give up her scheme easily. She was Carlos's mother and in time she must prevail. Jan buried her head in her hands; she wanted to be free of Carlos and his crazy idea, didn't she? Why then, when it seemed likely to happen, was she so miserable?

She looked at her reflection in the mirror and dusted delicate blue shadow on her eyelids, rubbed moisture lotion into her pale skin and outlined her lips with a soft pink lipstick. It was no use deluding herself any longer. She no longer wanted to be free of Carlos; she loved him too much. She met her startled eyes in the glass. Love? She loved Carlos? How could it have happened? She didn't even like him, but perhaps you didn't have to admire someone to want to possess and be possessed by him. She shook her head. It wasn't love; she wanted to sleep with him and if she did it would fade rapidly, but the solution was much too drastic. Her lips twisted in a wry smile. Who was she trying to kid? Desire, lust, call it what you will; she had still been stupid enough to fall in love with a man who despised her. No wonder she hadn't liked Alva kissing him; she had been jealous. She no longer wanted to leave him. She wanted to bind him to her so he would never want to leave her.

Her breath caught on a sob. It was madness to love a man like Carlos. In the ordinary way he wouldn't have given her a second thought. He was a very wealthy man, the owner of vast estates in Spain and the head of an old family, and as if that wasn't enough he was an astute businessman with interests in several countries, while she was a very ordinary girl with a small talent for drawing, and into the bargain he thought she was a thief.

She got up slowly and moved towards her dress spread out on the bed. Madness or not, it was too late; she loved Carlos with every nerve and fibre of her body. If she

were never to see him again he would be for ever fresh in
her memory, his every feature, the feel of his hand on
her arm, his mouth on hers, the individual aroma
composed of fresh linen, aftershave and the essential
man, would always be with her wherever she happened
to be. She would find herself listening for his step and
gazing after every tall, dark man she saw in the empty
years when his need of her was over. How she would bear
it when that time came she didn't know, and she
couldn't allow herself to dwell on it now or she would be
unable to play her part this evening.

Was it possible that Carlos would come to love her
in time? There had been moments during the last
weeks when she had thought he was softening towards
her, only to be brought up against his loathing for what
he thought she was. It was an impossible dream,
he couldn't love a thief, but if she could clear her
name ... Jan's breath quickened as she thought of how
Carlos would look at her then. He wouldn't love her, but
at least he would respect her. She felt an icy emptiness.
Carlos regarded her as little better than a prostitute and a
criminal.

She would try once more to talk to Wade. If she told
him how miserable the situation made her, surely he
would be able to do something to prove her innocence?
She knew instinctively that he could tell Carlos the
truth. The brightness went from her eyes. Wade didn't
love her and he would do nothing if it would implicate
his friends. It could also implicate Wade himself but she
must try; she would phone him tomorrow.

Jan sank down on the bed, her head in her hands. She
didn't want Carlos's respect, only his love. No, that
wouldn't satisfy her for long; she did want his respect
and everything else he had to give. She wouldn't be

happy with less than the complete man. She didn't know why he was so bitter and cynical about love, believing only in sexual satisfaction, but she didn't think she could settle for that. She wanted to give him everything and receive as much from him.

She stepped into her dress, smoothing the soft material over her hips. It was cut very simply with a modest neckline and full sleeves caught into a band of heavy coffee-coloured lace at the wrists, repeated at the narrow waist. The pale yellow matched her hair almost exactly, and Carlos's deep voice murmured his appreciation as he came up behind her. Jan, balanced on one foot while slipping into matching high-heeled sandals, lost her balance and fell into his arms. He kissed her, his mouth hard against her soft lips.

'I much prefer this scene to the last one I encountered in this room.' He cast a keen glance round him. 'I trust my mother and Alva have repaired the mischief they did to your clothes, Jacinta?'

'They were annoyed, Carlos, and rightly so. It isn't correct for you to expect your mother to accept your mistress.'

Carlos's mouth hardened into a straight line and his eyes narrowed. 'This is my house, Jacinta, and while my family are welcome here I will not allow any of them to dictate my actions. Neither will I allow you to censure me, is that quite clear?'

'It is, but I still think you are making a mistake. Your mother isn't going to acknowledge me as any kind of obstacle to her plans, and why should she? Mistresses are expendable in any language.'

'So that is your opinion,' Carlos said as they went downstairs. 'It is not mine and time will prove that I am right.' Jan held back the retort she wanted to make as he

stood aside for her to proceed him into the sitting-room.
Señora del Raimondes and Alva were already there.
Alva, seated on a small settee, looked lovely. Her red
dress was perhaps a bit elaborate for a quiet dinner at
home but the colour suited her, and the low neckline
showed the curve of her breasts to advantage. A bracelet
set with rubies matching those in her earrings flashed as
she held out her hand to Carlos, smiling at him, a warm
invitation in her eyes.

The *señora* came rapidly across to him from the alcove
where she had been examining the figures Jan had
arranged with such loving care.

'I have been looking at those ornaments and I find
them very poor. I will send you a collection of Lladro
and you can throw those away or give them to Miss
Shelley as a leaving present.'

'Jacinta is not leaving, Mother, and the figures are
very good ones and extremely valuable, as I am sure you
know.'

'Spanish figures are better,' Alva said, patting the seat
beside her. 'Sit by me, Carlos, and tell me why you have
bought a house in England when your mother tells me
you have a perfectly good flat.'

CHAPTER SEVEN

THAT had set the pattern for the rest of the evening. Alva had gone out of her way to be pleasant to Jan, sitting beside her on the settee and admiring her dress.

'The colour is right for you,' she said touching her own red satin dress with complacent fingers. 'You are so pale, but for me the colours of fire are better.' It sounded complimentary but the look she turned on Jan said the opposite. Her smile flashed again as Carlos strolled over to them and she was very careful to act as if Jan was her friend while he was near, but his mother treated her as if she wasn't there and Jan watched Carlos grow more and more angry until by the time his guests went to bed he was livid, his temper white-hot and looking for a target.

Jan excused herself and almost ran upstairs. Carlos was hard enough to deal with in normal circumstances but after the last few hours, when his mother had ignored everything he had said about treating Jan with respect, he was far too much for her to handle.

She could sympathise with him; he was under extreme pressure to marry Alva. Jan had no doubt at all that his mother loved him but she wanted to see her only son settled. His grandfather wanted a great-grandchild to carry on the family name, and his mother was determined to do her best to see he had his wish. Jan was in the way and the *señora* would remove her at any cost.

Next morning Jan was still determined to telephone to Spain. The *señora* and Alva were breakfasting in bed and Carlos had taken himself to the village. He had invited Jan to go with him and he had given her a look that made her shiver when she refused. She sat in Carlos's chair in his study, the telephone in front of her on the desk that, like the man who owned it, was strong and handsome.

She stretched out a hand and picked up the receiver and started to dial the number of the Spanish pottery. She was connected almost at once. The same voice as before answered her in Spanish, changing to English when Jan asked for Wade.

A hand clamped over hers and a decisive voice spoke briefly in Spanish before the phone was banged down. Jan cried out as Carlos dragged her from his chair with little regard to hurting her.

'You were phoning your lover, weren't you?' he snarled. 'I knew you were up to mischief when you wouldn't come with me to the village.' Jan flinched away from the rage in his eyes, a pulse in her throat beating so hard she could hardly speak. She forced her trembling limbs to hold her upright and was pleased to find her voice didn't falter.

'I was phoning Wade, yes. I wanted to ask him to clear up this muddle over the theft of your glaze.'

'You think he would and could do that?' Carlos's cold tones barely hid the fire that raged underneath.

'I sincerely hope he would and I know he could,' she answered quietly.

'Then you know more than he does. Felton assured me that it was your mistake with the names Johns and Johnson, not his, and I believe him.'

'Why should you believe Wade and not me?' Jan cried, and for a moment the lines of his mouth relaxed before curving in a sneer.

'I believe any man before a woman,' he grated. 'All your sex lie when it suits them to do so, and as for you, you can't even be honest enough to admit you want me.'

'As you want me,' Jan returned, her voice low and

husky. His challenge had made her aware of how much she craved his kisses. She flung her head back, her hair catching the light from the window. 'You do want me,' she said, growing bolder at the flame that sprang to life in his eyes as he touched her hair, curling it round his fingers. 'You can't deny it, can you?' she mocked. 'You want to make love to me against all your principles.'

'Yes, damn you, and I will, here and now.' Jan stared up at him, her excitement draining away. He reached for her slowly, taking pleasure in the fear evident in her white face.

'You can't, Carlos. Someone could come in.'

'Not if I lock the door.' He grasped her arm as she would have dashed past him and pushed her into a chair. He strolled deliberately to the door while Jan glared at him, her eyes huge, and just as deliberately he stretched out his hand to the door.

It opened before he could touch it and Alva appeared, her sulky expression vanishing as she saw Carlos. Jan slipped out of the room, evading Carlos's grasp. That had been a narrow escape. If Carlos had made love to her she very much feared she wouldn't have been able to hide her love for him. She shivered; he must never know or he would be able to exact a revenge far greater than just making her work hard.

The next few days were surprisingly calm and Jan tried not to think that a storm could be waiting just over the horizon. Carlos took his guests over the pottery and to Matlock. Jan refused to accompany them on either occasion. Carlos raised an eyebrow when she pleaded a headache the first time but he didn't question her, and she was grateful for the sensitivity he displayed, knowing she wouldn't want to see her old workmates and be subjected to their curiosity. The second time he wasn't at all understanding. He followed her to the long light room at the top of the house which she had commandeered as a studio and stood over her, overwhelming her even in the large attic.

'I want you to come with us,' he said and Jan, melting as she always did whenever she was near him, stiffened. He was ordering, not asking, and it was too much. It wasn't only Carlos who had been subjected to pressure. She had received her fair share, both from his mother and from Alva, who lost no chance of sly insinuation aimed at undermining Jan's confidence, but only when they were alone; when Carlos was present she treated Jan as her best friend. If only she knew, Jan thought bleakly, that I have no confidence at all where Carlos is concerned, only fears and apprehensions.

'I am going to work on the second series of the plates, Carlos. I want to get them finished.'

'They can wait another day. I won't take excuses, Jacinta, you are coming. Get ready to leave in half an hour.' He ran downstairs and Jan heard him calling Alva. She locked the door and returned to her painting, remaining impervious to the messages she received from Carlos by way of the maid and to Carlos himself when he came again and banged on the door.

'Go away, Carlos,' she said, feeling in every nerve his shock at such an answer. After a moment he went and Jan slid down in her chair as far as it would let her. She wanted to get up and run after him, to ask him to forgive her and take her with him, but as she unlocked the door she heard the car start and knew she was too late. Needless to say she didn't get much work done and not until she heard the car return two hours later was she able to put any enthusiasm into her painting.

She forced herself to concentrate and was taken by surprise as Carlos entered the room, and taking no heed of any damage he might do to her work, pulled her away from the desk and spun her round to face him.

'Do not ever lock yourself away from me again,' he grated, his eyes like black jet in a grim hard face. 'Do you hear me, Jacinta?'

'I can't fail to hear you. If you shout much louder everyone in the house will come running.'

He held her to him, his arms closing round her like a vice.

'Next time I ask you to come with me you will come, wherever it is.' He gave her a sharp shake before bringing his head down in a hard punishing kiss. Jan pushed her hands against his shoulders but the scent and feel of him, even through the shirt he wore, made a mockery of her defences and her fingers uncurled and crept round his neck. She returned his kiss, pressing as close to him as she could get and he groaned.

'*Dios*, why did you choose this room Jacinta? There isn't even a rug.'

The fumes of desire slowly clearing from her head, Jan put her hand on his as he caressed her breast, the touch of his fingers on the sensitive tip making her quiver.

'Let me go, Carlos. This isn't in our agreement. I should have come with you to Matlock but I had had enough of Alva for one day.' The mention of the Spanish girl brought Carlos's head up and he loosened his grip.

'I, too, have had enough of Alva. Did you have to mention her now, Jacinta?' He caught her to him again. 'Come with me to our suite; I can't stand out against you any longer. I want you so very badly, I have never wanted any woman as much.'

Jan wanted him quite as much and her heart missed a beat as she thought of her cool and lovely bedroom and the wide bed it held and for a moment she wavered, but the look of anger and self-disgust she saw in his eyes before his lashes shielded them strengthened her resolve.

'You know the answer is no, Carlos. I won't be used as a hair shirt,' she said with a steadiness she didn't feel. 'You may be able to throw your principles to the winds but I don't care to be the object of your lust.' She saw the flash of anger in his eyes and moved quickly to the door. She would feel safer downstairs; even Alva's presence would be welcome. Carlos's temper was at flash point and it wouldn't take much to drive him to do something they would both regret.

'How did your trip go?' she asked lightly as she walked into the small dining-room, where she was glad to see Betty had already set the tea tray.

'It was a disaster,' Carlos said bluntly, sitting down heavily in a honey-coloured cane chair. 'Alva and my mother are not nature lovers. The beauties of rivers and hills leave them cold, and I am informed that the Matlock shops leave much to be desired.'

'Oh dear, I am sorry,' Jan said, hardly able to suppress a chuckle.

'No, you are not, you horrible girl, you knew exactly how it would be.'

Jan grinned at him. 'Why did you think I refused to come?' She widened her eyes innocently. 'Tell me, did Alva wear those six-inch heels she favours?'

'She did, you brat, and so did my mother, and they both wore tight skirts. It was murder, particularly when it came to the crossing stones over the river.'

Jan could hold back no longer. She put the teapot down and laughed until her sides ached. The picture of the chic Alva and his elegant mother trying to negotiate the river by way of the flat stones with the water rushing round their feet was too exquisite for words. Carlos's laughter mingled with hers and he too saw how funny it must have looked, and they were both helpless when

Alva swept in, a look of disdain on her face as she saw them holding on to each other, tears of mirth streaming down their faces, the relief of the tension of the last few minutes making the incident seem far more humorous than it was.

'Is there something funny?' Alva wanted to know and she stared blankly when they laughed even harder.

At least it had been a bright note, even overriding the *señora's* criticism of the lovely little room.

'I do not like to eat in such a place,' she had said, looking round as if the fresh white paint and primrose carpet and curtains, the hanging baskets of plants and the containers of flowers and foliage standing in every corner were beneath her notice.

'Why, Carlos, have you not a proper dining-room?'

'We have, Mother, but it needs refurnishing and we both prefer this room.'

The *señora* had looked down her nose but to Jan's relief the conversation had passed on to neutral subjects.

Jan sat at her desk the next morning and sighed with satisfaction as she put the finishing touches to her picture of a red squirrel eating a nut while sitting on the branch of a small tree, its leaves young and shrilly green, while below primroses clustered amongst silvery ferns. Carlos had said she should paint foreign butterflies but Jan preferred the home-grown beauty of woods and fields. If Carlos didn't like her ideas he could get another artist.

At least she had achieved something. Alva had persuaded Carlos to take her into Derby and she supposed his mother had gone with them. The thought of the beautiful dark girl seated next to Carlos in the close confines of his car made her deeply unhappy, but this time he hadn't suggested Jan should join them.

She put her elbows on the desk, propped her head on her cupped hands and gazed out of the window. Beyond the formal rose garden, ablaze with colour, a line of hills met the horizon. A small aircraft drifted soundlessly across and out of her vision and Jan thought how peaceful it would be to be able to fly away from her troubles.

Would she really want to fly away if it meant leaving Carlos behind? She knew she wouldn't. Without knowing how it had happened she was committed to Carlos and she would stay as long as he needed her, no matter how many difficulties his mother and Alva put in her path. With that resolved she should have felt happier, but the plain fact remained that Carlos didn't really want her. He needed her to thwart his family's plans but he didn't love her and for her an affair wouldn't be enough. She needed to love and to be loved and as Carlos was the only man for whom she would ever feel deeply the future looked bleak.

The door opening broke into her thoughts and Jan turned to see Alva, in a smart black silk suit and her usual high-heeled shoes, saunter into the room.

'So this is where you are,' she said. 'Carlos say you are good artist, I come to see.' She looked at the painting placed on one side to dry and Jan wanted to shield it from her.

'That is not much,' Alva said. 'What good is a tree rat and a common flower?'

'It is not meant to be a great work of art. It is intended for a plate, one of a series,' Jan said, her voice harsh with anger at the other girl's rudeness.

'I would not spend on such a thing. You waste your time, and Carlos is foolish if he makes your plates.' She leaned against the desk, a sneer on her full lips.

'You didn't come here just to tell me you don't like my

work. What do you want, Alva?' Jan asked, the tight hold she was keeping on her temper making her nerves scream in protest.

'You are right, I wouldn't waste my time so. I have come to tell you to go. You should not be here; it is not well that you flaunt yourself in Carlos's house.' She leaned towards Jan with what she intended to be an understanding smile.

'I am modern woman, I understand these things. Carlos is much man, I do not care if he has you, as you English say, on the side, as long as you are away from this house.' Jan gasped with shock; she couldn't have heard Alva properly. Either that or the girl didn't know what she was saying.

'I think you haven't used the right words, Alva,' she said carefully. 'You couldn't mean that the way it sounded.'

Alva laughed stridently and Jan had a preview of the hard, selfish woman she would one day become.

'I know very well what I say. I do not care if you are Carlos's mistress as long as I and the friends I will make after we are married do not see you. Carlos can buy small suitable house some distance from here, perhaps in London. Yes, that would be best. He can hide you in London and I shall not mind if he journeys to see you once or twice a month.'

'So kind of you,' Jan said faintly, feeling as if she were in the middle of a nightmare.

'I am kind. Many wives would not be so good to their husband's woman but I will have what I want: the position as Carlos's wife and the things he can give me. I do not begrudge you a small place and a little of his company and a small piece of jewellery now and then, on your birthday and at Christmas perhaps.' So the jewellery Carlos had given her hadn't gone unnoticed, Jan thought.

'It could be good thing for me. Carlos is passionate man; I do not think I like that. He will want an heir and I will do my duty in that way, but if he wants more children he can look to you.'

Jan felt hysteria rising in her throat and knew that if Alva stayed she would scream and throw the nearest thing at her. She walked unsteadily to the door and opened it, but Alva hadn't finished.

'You agree, I am generous?' she said with one of her complacent smiles that made Jan feel ill. 'So you will go at once.' She looked at Jan as if expecting her to leave there and then but Jan met her eyes unflinchingly and it was Alva who looked away.

'You go,' she repeated. 'Carlos's mother says you are not wanted here.'

She walked out of the room. Jan heard her running downstairs and wished uncharitably that she would sprain her ankle in the unsuitable shoes she persisted in wearing.

The cheerful studio was no longer a refuge and Jan went to her room. She ran a hot bath and lay in it for a long time, and gradually the infamous suggestions and the venom with which they were made started to recede from her mind. What had made Alva say such things? She must know Carlos would be dreadfully angry if she told him. Or he would be if he believed her, but would he? He had known Alva for years and Jan only for a matter of weeks and she mustn't forget he still thought she was a thief.

She climbed out of the cooling water and dried herself thoughtfully. There was nothing to be gained by telling Carlos about the ideas Alva had cooked up; rather there could be a great deal to lose. Put into words it would sound as if she were trying to blacken Alva in his eyes. No wife in her right senses would condone such a plan.

Jan put on a rose-pink dress of fine silk with wide shoulder straps above the straight-cut bodice. Its full skirt reached mid-calf and her waist was clasped by a gold chain-belt matching her sandals. She let her hair loose and dusted her eyelids with pale violet shadow that deepened the colour of her eyes. She hesitated over jewellery and decided against the diamond pendant Carlos had given her. She had nothing else except some costume jewellery, and against the diamonds and rubies Alva wore they would look doubly false.

Carlos came in as she took a last look in her full-length mirror. He kissed her, then held her at arm's length.

'You are very beautiful,' he said huskily. 'I have missed you, you should have come with us.'

'You didn't ask me,' Jan retorted and scowled as he laughed.

'I think you also have missed me,' he said and kissed her again. He turned her round and, as once before, Jan felt the weight of a chain round her neck. She looked in the mirror and cried out with delight. Pink diamonds gleamed in a delicate gold setting, the colour and sparkle enhancing her violet eyes to a depth she hadn't known they held.

'You are pleased?' Carlos kissed her throat, his lips caressing her warm skin.

'It is lovely, Carlos, but I can't accept it, you know I can't.'

'I know nothing of the kind,' his eyes darkened and his fingers bit into her shoulders. 'I thought it was decided between us that you wear what I want you to wear.'

'You decided, Carlos, but I think this is going too far. I may not know anything about diamonds but I do know rose-coloured ones are very rare and very valuable.'

'Worth a king's ransom and worth every penny to adorn such beauty.'

Jan looked at him sharply, suspecting he was mocking her, but his expression was sincere and his eyes held a flame of desire that made her feel weak. His mouth curled and only now could she detect a trace of amusement.

'It is also necessary to convince my mother and Alva that I value you above any wife.'

'Would it be so terrible for you to conform to your family's wishes, Carlos?' she asked softly, holding her breath as she waited for his reply. Carlos gave her a small box and watched while she opened it and took out the earrings it contained. They matched the necklace, and without more argument Jan put them in her ears.

'Perfect,' Carlos said. His eyes met hers in the mirror and he frowned. 'The answer to your question regarding myself and marriage is yes, it would be a disaster. I shall not marry. I do not wish to be tied to one woman, but that does not mean I won't treat any woman I have as well as I can for as long as I want her.' He touched the sparkling stones in her ear. 'When I decide the time has come when we shall no longer live a lie I will cherish you as long as the desire we feel for each other lasts. I am not ungenerous, as I think I have already proved, and anything I give you is yours. Many marriages are made on a less secure footing than that, Jacinta, and many of them are over in a very short time.'

'You don't include children in your scheme?' Jan said, a heavy weight of despair centred in her breast making it difficult for her to speak.

'I see no reason to have children. I am not so vain that I think my genes are so remarkable they must be passed on to future generations.' He paused, his eyes hooded.

'Well, Jacinta,' he asked softly. 'Will you be my love on my terms? I promise you, you won't regret it.' He stretched out his hand, but when he would have pulled her to him Jan stepped back.

'No, Carlos, to me your terms are unacceptable.' She kept her voice low, but inside she was crying for the death of her dreams. She walked past him but a hand on her arm brought her to a halt.

'Think well before you decide, Jacinta. I will see you are taken care of after we part. Unless you want to you will not need to work again.'

Jan rounded on him, her eyes flashing, her head back.

'Money!' she spat out. 'That's all you know. I don't need to think, Carlos. I wouldn't become your mistress if you gave me the Crown Jewels. You and Alva deserve each other, and as this farce is about over you will have to fight your own battles from now on.'

'What do you mean by that? I knew something was wrong as soon as I came into the room. I thought it was pique because I didn't ask you to accompany me to Derby, but it is far more than that, isn't it? I insist you tell me.'

Her resolve not to tell Carlos of Alva's visit to her studio and her outrageous suggestions dissolved like mist and Jan related shortly and to the point Alva's solution to the problem as she saw it. For a moment Carlos was speechless, then he started to laugh.

'Oh, poor Jacinta, what a day you have had. First Alva, now me, both, it seems, after the same thing.'

'I am glad you find it amusing. I think you are both disgusting and thoroughly immoral.'

'Practical, Jacinta, and, as Alva says, modern.' He burst out laughing again and Jan walked out of the room. He caught her up before she entered the drawing-room.

'Our original agreement still stands, Jacinta, and I

shall have you for as long as I want you. I shall soon overcome your scruples.'

Jan tossed her head and marched into the room, not at all certain that he couldn't do just as he had said he would.

CHAPTER EIGHT

A WEEK went by and Jan began to forget both Alva's plan that she leave the house and the way Carlos had received the idea. It had continued to amuse him for the rest of the day. Every time Jan looked in his direction he had grinned at her till Alva asked petulantly what the joke was and could she share it? That had started him laughing and Jan, thoroughly fed up with all of them, had said goodnight and gone to bed.

Several times since then Alva had looked at her enquiringly, but Jan had ignored her, making sure she wasn't alone with the Spanish girl. She would have wanted to laugh at the frustration on Alva's placid features, as she forced herself to be pleasant to Jan in front of Carlos, if the urge to cry hadn't been greater. Alva had been more persistent during the last two days but Jan had managed to avoid her, until one evening she went down to dinner to find Alva waiting for her. Jan strolled across the room and poured out a glass of sherry, raising her glass enquiringly at Alva.

'No, I thank you,' Alva said primly. 'I prefer to wait until Carlos asks me. He is the master here.' Jan refrained from saying that Carlos had stressed more than once that she was the mistress, and strolled over to the window seat, hoping that Carlos or even his mother would come in. She didn't want another of Alva's suggestions.

'I think it is time you told me your plans to leave here for London,' Alva said. Jan glanced at her; she looked

very suitable to be the wife of a rich man. Her dress, in
her favourite red, was an expensive model and it showed
off her rather lush figure. It was rather low cut for an
informal evening and she had been heavy-handed with
the diamonds, but there was no doubt she was just what
Carlos's family wanted. Jan touched her cream chiffon
dress. Against the side of Alva's gown it was simplicity
itself but she liked it and Carlos's eyes had gleamed with
appreciation when he came into the bedroom as she was
leaving.

'I have no plans of any kind Alva,' she said quietly.

The Spanish girl's lips tightened into a straight line.
'We decided you should go to London.'

'I decided nothing of the kind,' Jan said shortly. Alva
was getting tiresome. 'If Carlos wants me to leave this
house he will say so.'

'You must tell him you want to go to London.'

'Why should I? I like it here, I like being mistress of
this house.' She looked at Alva mischievously. 'I also like
being Carlos's mistress.'

'I am very pleased to hear you say that, my Jacinta.'
Carlos's deep voice drowned Alva's gasp and Jan got
slowly to her feet as he came across the room. His lips
were warm and possessive and he took no notice of Alva
saying his name in an outraged squeal or the way Jan
tried to pull free. He dealt with her rebellion by
tightening his arm round her waist till she felt she was
welded to him. He thrust his other hand into her coil of
hair and proceeded to kiss her until she leaned against
him, trembling so much she couldn't have stood without
his support.

By the time he raised his head Jan had forgotten where
she was, forgotten everything but the man who could

make her body respond to his in such a way that she was part of him. A low laugh brought her back to the present and she realised she had undone two buttons of his shirt and that her strap had slipped from her shoulder and her hair was falling down.

She looked past Carlos to meet the blazing fury of Alva's black eyes and she blushed and drew away from him.

'I do not think this is the time or place for such an exhibition,' the *señora* said. Jan hadn't heard her come in, but then she wouldn't have heard a bomb going off. Carlos and his kiss had filled her world to the exclusion of everything else.

'I did not think you so dishonourable, my son, as to make love to your mistress in front of Alva.'

Carlos pulled Jan's strap back on to her shoulder, an intimate gesture that brought a snort of disgust from his mother, and did up his buttons, not in the least put out at his mother's censure.

'I was not making love, Mother,' he said mildly. 'Only kissing Jacinta. I have not seen her for at least three hours.'

'That is no excuse, Carlos. Alva is a young girl and your guest; she should not be subjected to such disgraceful scenes.'

'It was only a kiss.' Carlos's tone was still mild but his eyes narrowed and Jan knew it wouldn't take much to make him explode.

Alva sidled up to him and put her hand on his arm, her lovely eyes gazing appealingly at him.

'I know how you feel, Carlos, and how your mother feels, and Jan agrees with me that a small flat in London where you can visit her would solve all our problems.'

Jan closed her eyes and gripped the back of a chair. A

small house was now a small flat; it would be a bedsitter
next. Alva had really put the match to the fire.

'A small flat in London? That is what you have
decided, have you, Alva?'

'It would be best, Carlos, and Jan thinks so, too,' Alva
said eagerly, both hands clasped round his arm. 'I am
thinking of Jacinta, Carlos. It can't be very pleasant for
her. I am sure a place of her own would be more to her
liking.' She pressed her lips to his cheek and looked at
him like a child who has said something clever.

Carlos removed her hands from his arm gently.

'You are mistaken, Alva. I distinctly heard Jan say she
liked being mistress here and, as I have tried to make
clear, Jan's place is in my home with me.' Carlos put his
arm round her waist and faced his guests. 'I will only say
this once,' he said, his voice dangerously low. 'Jacinta
will stay here as long as I say; there is no question of her
moving to London or anywhere else. If you don't like
the position then I suggest you both leave.'

He pulled Jan out of the room and out of the house
and practically ran with her to his car. He pushed her
into the passenger seat and, while she was still trying to
catch her breath, leaped in and roared down the drive.
Jan looked back. The *señora* and Alva were silhouetted
against the lights from the hall and Jan wondered what
they were thinking about as they saw them leave.

'Where are we going?' she asked after they had been
driving for some time. Their first furious speed had
slowed down to a steady pace and for the last ten minutes
they had been travelling down winding country lanes,
quiet and beautiful in the soft evening light. He didn't
answer but after a few minutes brought the car to a stop
on top of a rise overlooking a peaceful valley.

'We aren't going anywhere in particular, I just had to

get out of that house.' He laughed angrily. 'I don't even know where we are and I snatched you away without your dinner.'

'I'm not very hungry,' Jan said. After the unpleasant scene back at the house she asked for nothing more than to sit here with Carlos and listen to the wind in the trees and the sleepy chirps of the birds as they settled down for the night.

'Do you begin to understand a little of the reason why I want you to act as my mistress? However determined a man is, he finds it hard to stand against an equally determined woman, and when there are two of them and one of them my mother . . .' He groaned and Jan found she sympathised deeply. Carlos undid her seatbelt and pulled her on to his knees, pushing his seat back and reclining it so they were half lying down.

'Don't fight me, Jacinta, just let me hold you. I need your calmness after the storm.'

Jan shivered, hearing him echo her own thoughts of a week ago was almost uncanny.

'I don't think the storm is over.' She rested her head on his shoulder, content to be in his arms. 'It's not working, Carlos. Your mother is determined to see you married, but I think it is Alva you should be wary of; she is a formidable opponent. She does not care how many affairs you have as long as she has your ring on her finger, and someone so—so detached and cold has a very strong hand.'

Carlos tilted her face up to his by tugging gently at her hair and kissed her, his lips dropping soft caresses on hers like wine into a precious glass.

'You could be right, Jacinta. I will have to consider further. I think Alva knows instinctively that we are putting on an act for her benefit.'

'In that case, the sooner it ceases the better.'

'Ah, no, my Jacinta. She only thinks, she can't know.'
He kissed her again, but something she had seen early in
the day flared to life in Jan's memory.

'She does know, Carlos,' she said, struggling back on
to her own seat. 'I saw her this morning talking to the
maid and I am almost sure Alva gave Betty some money.
I didn't think anything at the time and it still could be
just a tip for looking after her clothes.'

Carlos brought his seat upright.

'What has Alva talking to Betty to do with her
knowing we are only acting?'

'Don't you see?' Jan pounded his knee with her fists.

'No, Jacinta, I do not see. Please explain.' He captured
her hands in his and laughed into her eyes.

'We use two rooms, Carlos, and until now it has not
occurred to me to make it look as if you shared my bed.'

'An error we must rectify. I thought I was fighting
fire with fire but now I find I hold only a candle,' Carlos
said thoughtfully as he started the car. 'Fasten your
seatbelt, *querida*. I will give our situation more thought,
but first we will have dinner.'

After dinner they started back and Jan, sleepy from
good food and the tension that being with Carlos
brought, didn't realise they weren't going home until
the car stopped before the pottery.

'What are we doing here, Carlos?' she said, looking up
at the building before them.

'I have something to show you. Come, Jacinta.' He
helped her out of her seat and escorted her past the gate
man who touched his cap in response to Carlos's,
'Shan't be long, George.'

They took the lift to the executive floor and Carlos
unlocked his office door and switched on the light. Jan

sat down by the desk, wondering what Carlos could want to show her. He twirled the combination of a small safe behind his desk, opened it and removed a box. He placed it on the desk and carefully took out a plate.

Jan cried out in delight. It was the first of her designs and it exceeded all her expectations.

'Your new glaze,' she breathed, her eyes on the plate where blue and gold butterflies seemed as if they would dart from the china at any moment. The picture of the vase she had seen had been lovely but the reality far exceeded it. There was a depth of colour that brought it to life, the dandelion flowers glowed and the dandelion clocks appeared to sway before a breeze, trembling on the brink of drifting away.

'So you like it,' Carlos said, his eyes on the girl in front of him. She was so engrossed and appeared genuinely surprised and pleased with the plate; it was hard to believe she had conspired to steal.

'Who could help but like it? Oh, Carlos, it's wonderful! Thank you for using it on my plate.'

'Compensates a little for the loss of the glaze?' Jan's head jerked up at the cynicism in his tone. She met his hard gaze fully.

'I had nothing to do with the attempt to steal it and although I am honoured you used it on my plate, nothing compensates for being called a thief.' She stood up and moved to the door. Carlos put the plate back in the safe and followed her. He acknowledged the porter's 'Goodnight' and held the car door for Jan without speaking a word.

The house was silent, with only the lights in the hall still burning when they returned. Jan murmured goodnight, refusing Carlos's offer of a drink, and ran quietly up to her room. She showered and slipped into the first nightdress she put her hands on. She grinned as it whispered round her, falling softly to her feet. She had to admit that the flimsy black silk held by two narrow straps over her shoulders flattered her skin and hair as none of the other gowns she owned could. It was too dramatic, she thought, as she slipped into bed. She felt as if she were taking part in a play; it was just the nightwear for a courtesan. If Alva could see her now she wouldn't be so sure she and Carlos didn't sleep together.

She put out the light and closed her eyes and immediately thoughts of Carlos and the plate he had shown her came into her mind. His new glaze made it more exquisite than she had ever dreamed it could be. How anyone could try to take advantage of something that must have cost Carlos hours of work she didn't know. She groaned, flinging her hand over her eyes. He thought she was mixed up in it and she couldn't bear it.

She loved him more and more every day. He was gradually becoming part of her and if she didn't get away from him soon she would be bound to him for ever. But Carlos didn't want her for ever, only until his family was off his back. He and Alva would make a good pair; both of them knew how to use other people to their own advantage. It would serve them both right if they did get married, but the thought of Carlos locked in a loveless marriage was too painful. She wanted him to be happy and with Alva he could only be miserable; he was too sensitive for someone who steamrollered her way through life.

She sighed. Things had seemed so simple, so straightforward, only a few weeks ago. She had thought she was in love with Wade but it was nothing more than a girl's dream of romance compared to the love she had for Carlos. He was as necessary to her as breathing, as much a part of her as her own limbs, and she couldn't imagine a life without him. But he didn't love her and she was in a prison of Carlos's making, one she didn't want to leave.

Why was Carlos so set against marriage? There was a core of bitterness deep inside him she hadn't been able to breach and perhaps never would. He didn't trust any woman. If she could find some way of making him see that there were many women worthy of his trust she would be happy, knowing she had restored his faith in mankind, or rather womankind. She twisted uneasily. She didn't care about any other woman; she wanted him to love and trust her, but he was as likely to trust the real thief as he would her.

A slight noise brought her back from the edge of sleep. Cool air as the bedclothes were lifted, to be replaced by warmth and a hard masculine body sliding in beside her, had her rolling to the other side of the bed in panic. A low chuckle and Carlos's arm round her waist bringing her back against him made her relax for a moment, her body recognising, even while her brain rejected him.

'Carlos, what are you doing here?' She pushed her hands against his shoulders in a vain attempt to ward him off.

'What does it seem like, *querida*?' he murmured, his voice weaving strands of gold round her senses. 'I have decided you have had enough time and I no longer wish to play games.'

'But you hate to touch me,' Jan gasped.

'That no longer seems important,' he said huskily. He pushed the wisp of silk down to her waist and lowered his head to her breast.

'You are so beautiful, Jacinta. Your skin is like starshine and your hair matches the moonlight that is streaming through the window. A man could drown in the deep pool of your eyes and your breasts are perfection.' He cupped first one breast, then the other, in his hand, kissing and tantalising the nipples with his tongue until they hardened to rosy peaks and Jan moaned as intense pleasure lanced through her. With an effort she didn't want to make she put a hand on either side of his head in an attempt to stop him.

'Don't, Carlos, I don't want you. Get out of my bed.'

'You do want me, Jacinta, as I want you, and I refuse to leave you until we have ascended the heights together.'

'No, Carlos. No, I won't be your mistress. I only said I would pretend.' She looked into his face so near her own and saw implacable determination, mingled with intense desire plain in his eyes.

'It would be rape.' She twisted under him as his weight came down on her.

'No, my Jacinta, it will not be rape. You are reluctant to acknowledge me as your master, but when it is so and we are one you will be happier than you have ever been. It is time you became a woman, and after tonight you will be ... my woman.'

All the time he was speaking in that deep murmur that was capable of sending her into a near trance, his hands were touching and caressing, exploring her secret places that no man had touched before, until, when his mouth descended on hers, Jan was holding him to her, her hands stroking and moving over his broad shoulders and chest with a sureness that was instinctive. He parted her thighs and Jan gasped and stiffened at the sharp, unexpected pain. He stilled momentarily, then started a rhythm that caught her up, whirling her to an ecstasy she had never believed possible.

They lived on another plane, among stars that exploded round them before tumbling, together, back to earth. Carlos kissed her tear-stained face and refused to let her pull away from him.

'You belong here,' he said pressing her head down on to his shoulder. 'Sleep, my Jacinta.'

She sighed and did as he had said, waking as the dawn light banished the moonbeams, to find her limbs still intertwined with his and his arm lying across her as possessively in sleep as it had while he was awake.

He looked just as dangerous asleep as he did when his eyes were open, and full understanding of what had happened between them brought the colour flooding into her face. What an idiot she had been to imagine she should escape him. It was she who had played with fire and she had only herself to blame now she had been burnt. It would have been very difficult to forget him if she had left before this had happened; now it would be impossible. A tear trickled down her cheek as she thought of the lonely years that lay ahead. Now Carlos had achieved his object he wouldn't want her for very long.

He could in truth flaunt her as his mistress in front of his mother and Alva and they, recognising the truth as surely as they had known the falsehood, would return to Spain and Carlos would be able to resume his life, free of permanent commitments. But for Jan life would never be the same. No man could ever take the place of the man sleeping by her side. No man could make her feel as he did. He was wound into the fabric of her life as surely as a thread was woven into a length of cloth. He was the earth, the moon, the sun of her existence and when he left her the stars would cease to shine. She couldn't think of her life without him. To be able to see him, to know he was in the same house, was joy unconfined, but now he had made her his in every way, just to be near him wouldn't be enough. She couldn't live with him knowing it was only a matter of time before he gave in to his mother and married Alva. When that day came she would die; she would walk, talk and breathe but everything she was and had ever hoped to be would perish.

Why, oh why, couldn't you have left me alone? she wanted to scream. She wouldn't let him touch her again, but the damage had been done. There was nothing left for her but to leave, now, while she still could. She eased her limbs carefully free of his and moved gently away from his constricting arm. One more effort and she would be free. She rolled over, feeling the edge of the bed under her. She had pulled the clothes away from her legs when Carlos muttered and, reaching out in his sleep, brought her back to her former position.

She caught her breath as her eyes met his. He was fully aware of what she was trying to do; he had probably been awake all the time she had been trying to escape.

'*Querida*, how lovely you are with your skin rosy with sleep, your eyes drowsy with dreams and your hair defying the greyness of the dawn.' His voice deepened. 'Why didn't you tell me it was your first time, Jacinta? I must have hurt you.'

'Only a little,' Jan faltered, unable to find the words of rejection she had wanted to hurl at him before he had opened his eyes and enmeshed her once again in the magic only he could weave.

'You weren't trying to leave me, were you?' he asked in the same languid tones. She looked up to find his eyes fixed on hers, a hard gleam in their dark depths.

'Leave you?' she stammered.

'Yes, *querida*. I had the impression you were getting out of bed and that, if I hadn't stopped you, you would have left the house without waiting to pack.' His mouth curled at the corners but the angry light in his eyes warned her to be careful.

'Why shouldn't I leave you?' she said, her own anger rising. 'You have what you want and there is no need for me to stay.'

'There is every need.' He stroked the hair from her hot face, his touch making her sensitive skin come alive, every nerve responding to him. 'You are forgetting Alva, I think, and you are forgetting what we have between us. The first time is not so good for a woman. You must let me show you how it can be, my Jacinta.' His hands and mouth cast their spell once again and Jan submitted with hardly a murmur and before long she was responding to him, glorying in the way her body fitted against his, loving his strength and the way he made her feel.

The climax, when it came, swept her to unknown peaks and afterwards she snuggled against him, her arms round his waist. He chuckled and slid one long muscular leg over hers.

'I don't think you want to run away from me now, Jacinta, but in case you have second thoughts I think you should know I sleep very lightly.'

Jan woke with a feeling of well-being. She stretched her arms above her head and heard a murmur of appreciation. She turned her head to see Carlos standing by the bed. He was fully dressed and for a moment she wondered what he was doing in her room. Then colour flooded into her face and she hastily pulled the sheet over her shoulders as she remembered the abandoned way they had made love a few hours ago.

'Too late for that, my Jacinta. I know your beautiful body as I know my own.'

'Don't say that,' Jan said, finding it difficult to speak. 'Last night was a mistake, I want to forget it. And don't call me "your Jacinta". Your mother and Alva aren't here.'

'You are my Jacinta, now. It will not pay you to forget that fact. Our pretence is real and we will keep it that way.'

'We will not.' Jan sat up, forgetting the sheet in her indignation.

'How will you stop me, my Jacinta?' he asked, his silky tone making her quiver. 'I have only to kiss you so, to touch you so, and you are ready for me.' He kissed her, his tongue flicking over her lips, and touched her breast, his fingers on her nipples making her shudder. Jan wanted to deny his words but her upbringing wouldn't allow such a blatant lie. 'You see, you can't deny what is between us. I would prove it to you all over again but we are already late for breakfast and we don't want Alva to come looking for us, do we?' His eyes narrowed. 'Perhaps that would not be a bad thing. I think I will join you and prove to Alva that she has no chance of becoming my bride.'

Jan clutched the sheet to her and slid out of bed.

'I don't think that would work at all, Carlos. It would embarrass me, not Alva. She wants to be your wife and a mistress is no obstacle in her eyes.' She seized her gown and made for the bathroom, hearing Carlos murmur,

'I begin to think you are right, *querida*,' as she closed the door firmly behind her.

They went down to breakfast together, Carlos's arm round Jan's waist despite her efforts to dislodge it. The *señora* regarded them with a frown but Alva smiled complacently at them both and Jan's heart sank. How could Carlos think he could beat Alva? She was like a rubber ball; as soon as you knocked her down she sprang up with renewed life.

Carlos passed Jan a plate of bacon and eggs and she began, absentmindedly, to eat. He sat down next to her and attacked his own breakfast. For once the *señora* didn't grumble about the lack of fresh rolls and Jan glanced up to see her reading a letter, a self-satisfied smile on her lips.

'The English have a saying, Mother, about the cat who has been at the cream. You have exactly that look on your face. Your letter must please you very much.' His mother looked up with a triumphant smile.

'It does please me, my son, especially as it will bring you to your senses.' She gave Jan a look so vicious that she choked over the tea she was drinking.

Carlos put down his knife and fork, and, stretching out a hand, tweaked the letter from his mother's grasp.

'Carlos, that is a private letter. Return it to me at once,' she said irritably. Carlos turned it over in his hand, frowning at the bold black handwriting.

'I think not, Mother. It is from my grandfather and as it concerns me I have the right to read it.' He moved it out of her reach and for all his seemingly frivolous attitude Jan had never seen him so furious.

'Before you say it is not fitting conduct for your son to read your letters without your permission, allow me to say I agree, but it is not fitting for you, my mother, to send tales to Spain about me, particularly as you know my grandfather is not in the best of health. However, I will not read your letter if you will tell me the contents.'

His mother calmly drank her coffee before answering him.

'I have every intention of doing so,' she said. 'The

chief information in the letter is the time of your
grandfather's arrival at this house.'

For a moment there was complete silence. Jan looked
at Alva to find she was gazing back at her with an
astonishment that mirrored her own. Carlos resumed his
breakfast and Jan saw the slightest trace of uneasiness
cross his features.

'So the old eagle comes, does he?' he said at length and
Jan, who had begun to relax, tensed again. The quiet
answer hid a menace she was thankful wasn't turned in
her direction. His mother faced him squarely, her hands
flat on the table, any pretence of eating thrown away.

'I have informed your grandfather of the situation
here. As you well know, he will not tolerate such
immoral behaviour, and in view of the state of his health
I think you would be wise to put matters in order before
he arrives in exactly . . .' she picked up the letter Carlos
had returned to her, 'in exactly one week's time.'

'How do you suggest I do that, Mother?' Carlos
enquired, his voice still very quiet.

Jan held her breath and knew that Alva was doing
exactly the same thing. It meant so much to both of
them, and for the first time she felt as one with the
Spanish girl who, after all, was only fighting for her
happiness. Carlos was also determined to have what he
wanted and not what anyone else thought he should
have. Jan cradled her cup in her hands, trying to draw
comfort from the warmth it held. The three of them
only wanted to be happy; it was a pity their ways were so
very different.

'You know how, Carlos, without me telling you. You
must get Miss Shelley out of the house and make sure
the servants do not even mention her name. Your
grandfather will also act, as will Alva and I, as if she had
never existed.' An icy shiver ran over Jan; she felt as if

she wasn't there. The *señora* had wiped her out of Carlos's life as if she had never been in it.

'If I don't choose to do as you suggest?' Carlos asked, and to Jan's surprise he sounded amused. His mother rose from the table and Jan admired the dignity which she could never hope to emulate.

'I think you will, Carlos. You would not forgive yourself if you were responsible for your grandfather's death, and the sight of your mistress in your house could cause a fatal heart attack.' She swept out of the room, followed by a self-satisfied Alva.

CHAPTER NINE

CARLOS leaned back in his chair and to Jan's astonishment laughed wholeheartedly.

'You have to admit my mother fights for what she wants,' he said when he could speak without chuckling.

'Is your grandfather really ill?'

'He has a heart condition which, as he is ninety, is not so surprising, and Mother is right when she says he would disapprove of things here, though whether it would upset him to the extent of another heart attack is open to question.'

'You can't risk that happening,' Jan cried.

'No, my Jacinta, I can't.' He looked at her, his eyes hooded, and leaning over her kissed her. 'Do not worry, *querida*, Grandfather will love you, as I do. It is only our modern relationship he will find impossible to forgive.'

The door of his study closed behind him and Jan wandered slowly up to her studio. She didn't feel like work, but even if she had to tear her efforts up at the end of the day it would be better than sitting wondering what Carlos was going to do.

The rest of the day proved as fruitless as she had feared and the days that followed were nearly as bad. She did manage to finish the second plate of her new series and hoped Carlos would think the animal designs as pleasing as the butterfly plates. This one depicted a rabbit sitting in long grass, alert to everything around him, while bright-eyed birds watched from a nearby bush. White star-like flowers picked up the colour of the

animal's bobtail and, though it was not as colourful as
the butterflies, Jan thought it peaceful and satisfying.

She put down her brush and wondered what she
should do now it was finished. She had ideas for several
more plates but the motivation was lacking. She felt as if
she were living in a vacuum devoid of all that makes life
interesting and worthwhile. Alva had a secret little smile
on her lips whenever Jan saw her and the *señora* looked
through her as if she were already out of the house.

As for Carlos, he was the biggest puzzle of all. His
expression gave nothing away and several times his
mother looked at him, a thoughtful frown on her face.
He was acting as if he were in complete control of his
world and he couldn't be, not with his grandfather due
to arrive in less than four days' time.

Jan drew a piece of paper towards her. It wasn't doing
any good to speculate on what would happen next
Saturday. She couldn't stay here but Carlos had said
nothing to her about leaving. Neither had he made love
to her again. In fact, he had hardly even spoken to her
and his kisses had been confined to one every morning
and evening, given in the presence of his mother and
Alva.

She tried to tell herself she was glad he hadn't come to
her again and that she was thankful to be spared the
effort of saying no, but deep down she was very
unhappy. She had been proved right; Carlos, having
once possessed her, didn't want her any more. She
fiercely suppressed the loss and desolation she felt every
time she thought of lying in his arms. The desolation
that swept over her as she remembered the way he had
made her feel was too powerful to be borne. It would
almost be a relief to leave, as she must do in a few days,
and she closed her mind to the thoughts of what would
happen to her once the door of Carlos's house closed

behind her for the last time. She would live, somehow; you didn't have to be happy to survive.

If she had any sense she would go now. She got up, then dropped back into her chair; she couldn't leave Carlos until he told her to go, she would have to hear him say the words. Jan buried her face in her hands. She could at least keep her self-respect if she cut the chains that bound her to him. She gave a strangled sob; far from loosening her bonds she was hugging them to her.

She looked down at the paper under her hand in amazement. She had unconsciously started to draw and the picture that stared up at her was Carlos, but Carlos in the form of an eagle. She gripped the edge of the paper to tear it up, but something stopped her and she examined it more closely. Carlos was thinly disguised as the lord of the skies; there was no mistaking his eyes or the expression on the eagle's face. Idly she sketched Carlos as a man beside the bird, putting them both against a background of towering mountains and dark ominous clouds. She noticed with interest that the man dominated the bird as Carlos dominated everyone and every creature he met.

The door opened and high heels tapped across the uncarpeted floor. Jan looked up, expecting to see Alva, but it was the *señora*, dressed in a superbly fitting black suit, who stood looking down at her, a contemptuous smile briefly curving her lips.

'So this is where you waste your time,' she said, gesturing imperiously for Jan to rise. For a moment Jan thought of sitting just where she was but there wasn't another chair in the room and the *señora* was Carlos's mother. She got up and offered her chair to the older woman.

'My son tells me you are an artist,' she said, seating herself and picking up the painting of the rabbit. Unlike

Alva, she seemed to like it, her eyebrows rising in surprise.

'I see he is right. I congratulate you, Miss Shelley, on your work, but not on your stubborn refusal to leave this house.' She put the painting down and leaned back, crossing shapely ankles. 'Find somewhere to sit, Miss Shelley. I do not wish to have a pain in my neck through looking up at you and what I have to say will take some time.' Jan sat on a corner of the desk and satisfaction showed in the *señora's* dark eyes.

'That is better. What will it take to get you away from here?' She shot the question so abruptly that Jan blinked.

'Carlos won't hear of me leaving,' Jan said slowly, anger making her heartbeat quicken.

'It will do you no good to stay, Miss Shelley. My son won't marry you.'

'He doesn't want to marry anyone, *señora*.'

'Has he told you why?' the *señora* asked smoothly. 'No, I thought not. It isn't something he talks about to every woman he takes to bed.' Jan stared at the woman seated so comfortably in her chair and felt anger lash her nerves at the way the *señora* had tried to put her in her place as just another woman Carlos chose to entertain him.

'Carlos will tell me what he wants me to know,' she said stiffly.

'Perhaps, but I think you should know why Carlos will only marry someone like Alva who will leave him free and not worry him with her demands for the love he can't give.'

'You think I would do that?'

'The question doesn't arise.' The *señora* looked at Jan with something like compassion. 'You are in love with

my son, are you not? Unfortunately Carlos has no love
to give you or any woman.' She smoothed a skirt that
was already wrinkle free.

'When he was barely twenty, Carlos fell in love with
an English girl who was staying with relatives near our
house in Spain. She was blonde, as you are, and like you
she fell in love with him, so much in love that she hardly
let him out of her sight. Carlos felt the same way about
her and for six months they forgot there were other
people in the world.' She passed her hand over her eyes
and Jan saw that she wasn't enjoying talking about
Carlos and his love.

'I thought it was unhealthy; they were obsessed with
each other. Carlos had to leave Spain for a few weeks on
urgent business so I took the opportunity of introducing
Alison to other men, older, more sophisticated and
above all richer than Carlos was then. The inevitable
happened and by the time Carlos came home with an
engagement ring in his pocket, Alison had gone.

'He was frantic for a time, but he flung himself into
building the Eagle Potteries into what they are today. He
delved into many other businesses and it is due to his
devotion to his work that the family has the standing and
wealth we have now.'

'Didn't you stop to think of how you were hurting
your son?' Jan said, her fingers gripping the edge of the
desk until they ached.

The *señora* lifted her head proudly.

'I was not sorry then, and I am not sorry now, that I
prevented my son marrying such a girl. She was not
worthy of him and the name he bears and neither are
you, Miss Shelley. Alva will make him a suitable wife
and with you out of the way he will soon become

resigned to the need for an heir to the empire he has built up.'

She looked at Jan expectantly. 'I realise you will need compensation for giving up all this ...' She waved a hand round the room. 'I will give you a reasonable amount to keep you until you get another position. I can't keep you in luxury and you must leave the jewellery Carlos gave you—it will suit Alva very well.'

Rage threatened to overwhelm Jan, rising in waves of furious colour to her face. Her pink diamonds wouldn't suit Alva at all and she wasn't going to have them.

'You might think it would be better if you took Alva's offer of a flat where Carlos could visit you. It wouldn't happen, Miss Shelley. Alva didn't mean what she said for a moment; no woman would.' Jan agreed with that. Alva's suggestion had only been window-dressing, a ruse to get Jan out of the house, and once out she would find ways to make sure Carlos didn't see her again.

'I know Alva has no intention of allowing me to remain in Carlos's life if they marry,' she said far more calmly than she felt. 'But it isn't what Alva wants that concerns me. As far as I am concerned, what Carlos says is law.' Jan heard her own words with surprise and alarm. When had she ever taken anyone's command as her law? She let her lashes shield her eyes. She had spoken nothing but the truth: what Carlos wanted she wanted; what he commanded she would do.

The *señora* got up, shaking her skirt free of imaginary creases.

'I am sorry you won't see reason, Miss Shelley. I repeat, my son won't marry you and when he and Alva are wed your position will be untenable.' She swept out of the room and Jan sank down in her chair. Carlos's mother was right, her position was already impossible, but there was nothing she could do. While Carlos wanted her she would stay.

She was sitting on a powder keg, Jan thought, as Wednesday drifted into Thursday and Carlos still said nothing about her moving out of his house. His mother grew more and more tight lipped and even Alva's confidence began to wane. Only Carlos seemed unperturbed by the steadily building atmosphere. Jan mutely asked him the questions she didn't dare voice as they sat opposite each other at dinner a scant few hours before his grandfather was due, only to have him return her gaze with dark eyes that stared into hers as if they were mere acquaintances with nothing between them more serious than a handshake.

She resolved to ask Carlos what he intended she should do without wasting any more time, but he proved as elusive as sand blown before a high wind and she went to bed still not knowing the answer. Her sleep was troubled and daylight was stealing through her window before she slept at all soundly. When she was awakened by a hand on her shoulder she turned over and murmured, 'go away'.

An anxious 'miss' brought her upright to see Betty standing by her bed, a cup of tea in her hand.

'Mr del Raimondes asked me to give you this, miss.' She handed Jan a sealed envelope and put the tea on the bedside table. 'He said it's urgent, miss,' she said as she closed the door behind her.

Jan held the note in her hand and frowned. Carlos hadn't slept with her again. He didn't seem interested any more and she thought that his disgust had surfaced again. Certainly during the last few days he had treated her as if she were his enemy and not the woman he had held in his arms and to whom he had made such

passionate love that it still made her shake whenever she
saw him. Now, instead of speaking to her, he had sent a
note.

She looked at it again and her lips quivered. Carlos, as
usual, didn't ask, he ordered. They were going out as
soon as she had had breakfast. 'Hurry, and wear
something pretty. Carlos,' the note stated and Jan could
hear him saying the words. She stared at it and
wondered what it could mean. She shrugged her
shoulders and decided on a shower for speed—she knew
Carlos would be quite capable of dressing her if she took
longer than he thought she should. They were going out.
Why, and where were they going?

Jan swung her legs out of bed, feeling the floor had
dropped from under her. Carlos's grandfather was due
and she had to be out of the house before he arrived.
They would be going to see the flat Carlos had found for
her and his male pride dictated the 'wear something
pretty' order. Jan bathed and dressed in a sleeveless silk
dress in the palest shade of primrose. She stepped into
high-heeled sandals in the same shade and picked up a
matching handbag. It promised to be very hot later on,
so she wouldn't need a coat. She looked in the long
mirror, noting without much interest that her hair
gleamed and curled round her shoulders as if it were
alive—or perhaps one of the moonbeams Carlos had
compared it to, she thought fancifully.

She took a last look round the room where she had lain
in Carlos's arms for one night and wondered if she
would ever see it again. A numbness, masking pain, stole
over her at the thought that this time she really was
leaving Carlos. Whatever he had arranged for her, this
was the end. She wouldn't live in any flat waiting for
him to come to her when he could spare the time. She

would go away, somewhere she could make a fresh start and try to forget that Carlos had ever entered her life.

He looked at his watch as she entered the dining-room and she wondered what she had done to merit his cold, assessing expression. She accepted the food he put before her, speculating, as she tried to eat, why he was so formally dressed. His pale grey suit made him look even more masculine than he usually did, moulding his broad shoulders to perfection and contrasting with his dark hair and eyes in a way that made her lose what little appetite she had.

He didn't appear to notice that she left most of her food on the plate, he seemed to be in a hurry and the moment she replaced her cup on its saucer he hurried her from the room, passing Alva in the doorway.

'Carlos where are you going?' she cried, holding her face up to him. He patted her shoulder, refusing her invitation to kiss her.

'I have an urgent appointment, Alva. Please tell Mother I don't know what time we shall return,' he said, whisking Jan across the hall and out of the house.

Once out of the grounds of Over Grange, Carlos's urgency vanished. He drove at moderate speed through the sweet-smelling country lanes until he came to a parking place overlooking fields and hills that appeared to be deserted.

'I thought you were in a hurry, Carlos?' Jan said after they had sat for several minutes in silence. It was a lovely day and she would have liked to walk over the low hills she could see in the distance with Carlos at her side. Perhaps they wouldn't reach the hills. Things tended to be further away than they looked, just as love and happiness seemed to be out of her reach.

Carlos had discarded his jacket and sat with one arm

on the steering wheel, leaning forward, as if he could see into the future and didn't like what he saw.

'You said you had an appointment, Carlos,' she prompted, laying a slim hand on his arm. He stiffened and moved so that her hand fell to the seat and Jan caught a glimpse of an icy anger before his lashes hooded his eyes. She shivered, she must have been mistaken, and the next moment she knew she was as Carlos smiled.

Jan trembled. Sitting so near to him made her want to be even nearer, to act the wanton and strip away the flimsy barriers of his shirt and her dress so that nothing was between them and only they and the desire they felt for each other existed. Carlos turned his dark eyes to her.

'Um? An appointment? Oh, yes, but not for an hour.'

'Then why the rush? Alva wanted to talk to you.'

'I did not wish to talk to her. I want to talk to you and make you understand why I won't be pressured into a marriage of my family's choosing.' Jan sat very still. Perhaps at last she was going to learn something about this man she loved and who was almost as big a mystery to her as he had been the first time she had met him.

'My father died when I was two,' he began. He slipped an arm round her shoulders and pulled her close to him. 'We may as well be comfortable,' he murmured.

'Go on with your story,' Jan said, deciding against her better judgement to stay where she was.

'My grandfather spoiled my father all his life. He gave in to his every whim and all he asked of him was that he should provide an heir. This he did, but he had no interest in either me or my mother. He was an international sportsman, a world-class skier, and sport was his whole life. He died at the height of his fame, a stupid accident in a car.'

'I am surprised your mother didn't marry again.'

'She did, and it was a disaster. It was a relief when her husband drank himself to death. He had thought he was on to a good thing but my mother had no money of her own. My grandfather made her an allowance on condition that he took complete charge of me, and this time he didn't repeat his mistake of spoiling the child; in fact, he went too far the other way.' Carlos twisted a lock of Jan's hair in his fingers.

'I was brought up as if I were a recruit in the army and taught that duty and the family interests must come first. It was also drilled into me that all women and most men are unreliable and traitors.'

'Your grandfather should be shot,' Jan said, indignation mixed with pity for the way a small child had been treated. She glanced at Carlos and he laughed.

'I am not my grandfather and he has since realised his mistake. All the same, he did such a good job that I set my face against marriage.'

'There was a time when you thought of marriage,' Jan murmured, almost to herself. Carlos drew in his breath sharply and Jan put her hand to her mouth in fear as he swung her round to face him, an icy glare in his dark eyes.

'Who has been talking to you?' he demanded and Jan shivered.

'Your mother told me about Alison. It does explain why you don't trust any woman and why you can't love anyone else.'

'*Dios*! What fools you women are! Do you really think I still pine after a stupid girl who went out of my life ten years ago? But you are right in one thing, she finished my grandfather's lessons on the hypocrisy of your sex. As for love——' He broke off, his brooding gaze fixed on Jan until she wanted to scream.

She wasn't at all sure he was over Alison; his bitterness against women seemed to say he still loved her. She caught a cynical gleam from dark eyes.

'Don't pity me, Jacinta. I can deal with your desire for me, but I don't need anyone's pity.'

'Not pity, Carlos. Sorrow that you will never know the depths of love or the warmth of a family of your own.' He smiled at her and Jan froze; she hated the devilish smile he produced when she angered him.

'I don't know what love is,' he said at last. 'My grandfather taught me extremely well, but a family could be another matter. The old devil is determined to change my mind for me, even going to the extent of recruiting my mother to his cause and giving Alva his blessing. He wants an heir, but if I obey him, what guarantee have I that my son would want to take over from me? He might take after my father who wanted nothing to do with any of the family enterprises.'

'You took over the del Raimondes empire,' Jan said. 'Why shouldn't your son do the same? And you could have more than one.'

'Spread my chances? That's an idea. How many do you think we should have, Jacinta? Three, four, or more?'

'Including girls, you mean?' Jan asked, entering into the game, caught up by the glow in Carlos's eyes and very relieved that his anger appeared to be over.

'Girls would be extra,' Carlos said with a wicked grin.

'Oh would they? I pity your poor wife.' She slanted a glance at him. 'None of this will happen will it, Carlos?' she said, sighing at the dream that never was.

'Why not, if you are willing?' He bent his head and his lips touched her cheek, leaving a trail of fire on their way to her lips.

He put Jan back into her seat and looked at her, his face expressionless.

'We are getting married today, Jacinta; it is all arranged. We are due at the register office in fifteen minutes,' he said in such a matter-of-fact tone that it didn't register in Jan's mind. He pulled his jacket towards him and, taking a small box from the pocket, opened it. Jan had just time to see a flash of light before the ring was on her finger. She stared in stunned amazement at the enormous emerald surrounded by diamonds on her left hand.

Automatically she started to pull it off but Carlos stopped her, his fingers gentle yet very firm. He held her hand and kissed the ring and then placed a light-as-air kiss in her palm, closing her fingers over it.

'You will have to transfer the ring to your other hand for the ceremony, Jacinta, but I want to see it on your finger until then.'

Jan tugged at her hand in vain and raised an angry face to his calm one.

'This joke has gone far enough, Carlos. You know very well you have no intention of marrying anyone. Or is this a rehearsal for asking Alva to marry you?' she said, white at the thought of him marrying Alva.

'Are you mad? I would no more marry that man-eating tiger than I would marry my grandfather. I have decided to do as the old man wants. He has been a hard, strong, proud man. Now he is old and tired but he is still proud; our marriage will make him happy.'

'I doubt that very much.' Jan said drily. 'If it were to take place he would view it with horror. Don't forget he believes me to be your mistress.'

'I shall explain,' Carlos said simply and Jan saw he

sincerely believed his grandfather would believe whatever he told him.

'There won't be anything to explain, Carlos. I am not
going to marry you. How can you think such a marriage
will succeed?' Carlos rubbed his fingertip over the
emerald on her hand.

'It stands as good a chance as any other marriage,
querida. More, I think than the ones entered into in a
love-clouded haze.'

'I believe in love,' Jan said defiantly.

'Certainly you do, most women do. But we have
something better; there is a flare of chemistry between
us that will give us much joy.' He tilted her chin and
looked into her stormy eyes. 'We will be married,
Jacinta.' He looked at her with such intensity that Jan
felt all defiance flow from her like water from a tilted cup
and that whatever he said would come true. She sat
quietly as he started the car and drove back into the
centre of the town. Just before they got out of the car, he
gave her a small white box. Jan, still in the daze he had
thrown her into, opened it and exclaimed in delight at
the spray of tiny cream orchids. Carlos produced an
emerald and diamond brooch in the shape of a butterfly
and deftly pinned the flowers to her dress, his fingers
lingering on the pulse in her throat as he kissed her
gently.

'Trust me, my Jacinta, please,' he said with such
sincerity that she responded wholeheartedly, returning
his kiss and going with him into the office without
protest. The registrar was waiting for them and it wasn't
until Carlos placed a heavy gold ring on her finger that
Jan really became aware of what was happening. Her
eyes widened in panic and she opened her lips to scream
a denial, but Carlos, holding tightly to the hand she

would have pulled free, caught her to him and kissed her
hard.

'It is too late now,' he murmured. 'You are my wife.'

Carlos's wife. Jan, feeling the weight of the rings on
her finger, couldn't believe it. She glanced fearfully at
the man who, driving the huge car with an ease she
envied, was her husband. They stopped for lunch at a
small wayside inn and she wondered what the sophisticated Carlos would think of pub food. To her surprise he
appeared to thoroughly enjoy the ploughman's lunch he
had ordered.

'We should have champagne, Jacinta, but we will
have it tonight with the wedding dinner Mrs Kent is
cooking for us.'

'How does she know?'

'She doesn't know what we are celebrating. I just
ordered a special dinner.'

'You were very sure of me, weren't you?' Jan asked, a
heavy weight settling on her chest.

'I was confident I could persuade you. Eat your lunch,
Jacinta. I don't want my bride fainting from hunger.'

Jan pushed her salad round the plate; it was
impossible for her to eat a thing. She picked up the glass
of white wine Carlos had ordered instead of champagne
and drained it. The whole thing was fantastic: the
ceremony, so different from the wedding she had once
dreamed of, and especially Carlos; he was not at all the
kind of bridegroom who had been part of those dreams.
He was lying back, apparently at ease with his world, but
underneath she sensed he was tense with something very
like rage. Why should he be angry? He had, as usual, had
his own way, but for a newly married man he looked far
from jubilant.

Something was very wrong and she bitterly regretted

allowing him to persuade her into marrying him.

'Why did you marry me, Carlos? Why me?' she cried, her voice rising as she tried to understand why a man who had said he would never marry had changed his mind so completely.

Carlos got up and held his hand out, and Jan allowed him to take her back to the car and sat quietly while he drove away, her heart heavy at the grim look in his eyes. He stopped the car at the same viewpoint where he had given her the emerald ring before their wedding. He reached for her but Jan put both hands flat on his chest, holding him away from her.

'You didn't want to marry anyone, Carlos so why?' she said again, knowing in advance she wouldn't like the answer.

'You are right, *querida*,' he said, his tone making mockery of the endearment. 'I didn't and don't want a wife but it is the only way to get peace both for my grandfather and myself. The old man will be pleased thinking he will have his heir in due course, and I am free to pursue my own life.'

'How can you marry someone you don't trust?'

He shrugged wide shoulders. 'I do not trust any woman, you least of all, but there is something in dealing with the devil, you know. Marriage will take the pressure from me and I shall be able to curtail any criminal tendencies you may still possess.'

The colour drained from Jan's face and she curled her hands into fists.

'What about me Carlos, what am I supposed to do?'

'You are my wife and you will act accordingly.'

'While you go your own way?'

'Just so, Jacinta. You are very quick.' He lifted an eyebrow. 'It won't be so bad. You will have everything you have ever wanted and you can continue to paint if you wish.'

'Why didn't you marry Alva? She would have suited you just as well and she would have been willing,' Jan said woodenly, feeling she knew just what novelists meant when they wrote of heartbreak.

'Are you saying you are not? I do not believe that and tonight I will prove it to you.' His arm tightened round her waist and she was pulled ruthlessly against him while he plundered her soft mouth with lips as relentless as the fingers biting into her side. Jan leaned against him, unable to withstand either the emotions he aroused or his superior strength.

He relaxed his hold and put her back in her seat, doing up the belt with hands that didn't have the slightest tremor, whereas Jan trembled from her head to her toes.

'The seats of a car are not right for what I have in mind,' he said huskily, and Jan twisted her hands in her lap at the picture of them lying, limbs intertwined, in the wide bed his words conjured up.

'We will go home now, Jacinta, and inform my mother of our marriage. After my grandfather's visit we will leave for our honeymoon. Please give some thought to where you would like to go.'

Jan tidied her hair as soon as her hands were steady enough to hold a comb, seeing with pleasure that the orchids had not been ruined by the force of Carlos's embrace. She renewed her lipstick, meeting a glance from Carlos that said it was a waste of time. She tossed her head and adjusted the neck of her dress. It wouldn't do to appear before Carlos's mother and Alva looking as if she had been rolling round in the back of a car. Her face grew warm as she realised that was exactly what had happened and that, if Carlos hadn't stopped, she would have done nothing to prevent them celebrating their wedding there and then.

She caught the sparkle of the emerald in her ring and the gleam of the wide gold band beneath it. She twisted it round her finger; it looked old and valuable, and was engraved with something she couldn't make out. Perhaps it was a coat of arms.

'It is an eagle, the family crest. That ring has been worn by del Raimondes brides for two hundred years.' Carlos spoke so quietly, Jan wasn't sure he had spoken. Her eyes flew to his.

'Stop it, Carlos, I don't like you reading my mind.'

'It comes naturally, *querida*, I am sure you can read mine if you try.' He looked at her briefly and Jan had a glimpse of such passion and desire she thought she would faint. Carlos nodded his head.

'I knew you could. It is a useful accomplishment between husband and wife.'

'Not so useful if one of us falls in love with someone else.' She laughed shakily, thinking he would laugh with her, but a demon looked out of the hooded eyes he turned to her.

He brought the car to a screaming halt and seized her roughly, his hands gripping her arms with fingers of steel.

'Don't even think of looking at another man, Jacinta, or you will be sorry to your dying day,' he grated.

'It was only a joke, Carlos. But why not? I am sure you will not deprive yourself . . .' Her voice tailed off before the sheer fury that radiated from him.

'I don't mean it Carlos,' she said hurriedly. She flung back her head. 'Only a Spaniard would talk of dying on his wedding day,' she said, trying to sound very much braver than she felt.

'Only an English woman would joke about infidelity on her wedding day,' he retorted. 'Make certain, my Jacinta, that it remains a joke.' He released her and she rubbed her arms, wincing at the pain.

'I hurt you, Jacinta. I am sorry, but you will not say such things again or you can expect more than a few bruises.' He started the car, and Jan tried to gather her shattered nerves together.

CHAPTER TEN

As soon as they stepped into the hall Jan knew that something was different. Carlos stopped short, a frown gathering his dark brows together, then an expression of sheer joy made his eyes glitter. He waved to a leather case that stood near the foot of the stairs.

'The old devil,' he said softly. 'He has stolen a march on us and arrived a day early. What a good thing, my Jacinta, that I have out-guessed him.'

He opened the drawing-room door, his arm firmly round Jan's waist. She saw, with relief, that the room held only two people. Señora del Raimondes got to her feet and almost ran to Carlos.

'Thank goodness you have returned, Carlos. Your grandfather is here. Get that woman out of the house unless you want to kill him.'

'My grandfather is much tougher than you give him credit for, Mother, and as I have said before, I will say who goes and who stays in my house.'

There was a definite warning in his tone but his mother wasn't in the mood to heed anything beyond the golden opportunity of getting rid of Jan. Alva sat like a satisfied cat expecting more cream as the *señora* unleashed a flood of Spanish.

'English, Mother. Jan can't understand Spanish, though I hope she will learn.' He smiled at Jan, touching her cheek with a long finger. 'I will see about a tutor for you and then, when we go to Spain to stay with grandfather, you will be able to understand and give orders to the servants.

'Give orders to my servants? Only your wife will do that, Carlos.'

Jan froze as a deep voice vibrant with anger made itself heard. Carlos turned round slowly, taking Jan with him, and she had all she could do to stand firm before the newcomer. That he looked every day of his ninety years, was her first thought, but his age only added to his formidable presence. Not quite as tall as his grandson, he had obviously been just as powerful at Carlos's age and even now he was upright and fit-looking. His black eyes mirrored the determination she had often seen in Carlos's and his white hair was still thick and healthy.

'Grandfather, I am pleased to see you in my home.' Carlos grasped the old man's hand in his and Jan could see there was a strong affection and respect between them. The old man had caught all the nuances in Carlos's reference to his home, but he chose to ignore them.

'I should be pleased to be in your house Carlos, except for that woman. Your mother has told me of the way you insist on keeping her here, even though she and your *novia* are here.' His brows lowered over hard eyes that bored into Jan. 'Young woman, if Carlos is blind to decency, I am sure you are not. I expect you to leave within the hour.'

Jan felt Carlos's fingers dig into her waist harder and harder as his grandfather was speaking. She dared not look at him, knowing only too well how livid he was at his grandfather telling him what to do in his own home. The old man continued to glare at them both, not in the least disconcerted by the unexploded bomb facing him in the form of his grandson. Jan held her breath but when Carlos did speak, after an unnerving silence, his voice was very quiet.

'You are my grandfather so I will not knock you down as I would any other man who has insulted Jacinta as you have.' He kissed Jan on her mouth, lingering for several moments, and she wondered why he didn't tell his family they were married.

'Carlos!' The old man's outraged roar made Carlos smile grimly as he raised his head. 'I never thought you would behave so badly in front of your wife-to-be,' he said. Carlos's eyes moved and he glanced at Alva, who ran over to him and smiled as if she were indeed his fiancée.

'Alva is not my fiancée, Grandfather,' Carlos said softly. 'At no time have I, or will I, ask her to marry me.' He raised an imperious hand as everyone started to speak. 'Even if I had wanted to marry Alva, it is now impossible. Jacinta and I were married this morning.' Into the stunned silence his words fell like poisoned drops into a cup. 'As you were under a misapprehension, Grandfather, I will not insist that you apologise for the way you have spoken to my wife. I will be as magnanimous to you, Mother, and to Alva, but in future you will remember who she is.'

He swept Jan out of the room and upstairs before any of the others could recover. Jan sat on Carlos's bed, where he had deposited her, feeling sick. It had been dreadful, although not so much in what was said or even the way they had spoken; everyone had been well controlled, perhaps too much so, while all the time daggers were being drawn.

'Change your dress, Jacinta, and freshen your make-up, and we will go down for tea. After that little fracas I could do with some.'

'A little fracas, is that what you call it? It was awful!

How can I face any of them again?'

'You can, Jacinta, and you will. Think how Alva would gloat if I made excuses for you.' Jan sighed and gave in. Carlos knew exactly what she was thinking; it was no use trying to conceal anything from him.

Tea was an amazingly peaceful time, as were the hours that followed. Jan, looking round the dinner-table, couldn't believe that the calm surface didn't mask hidden shoals and she quivered with nerves, waiting for rocks to hole her frail craft, as she lifted the finely cut glass and sipped the delicate white wine.

At least Carlos had driven Wade out of her mind. No doubt she could have been quietly happy with him or would she have been conscious of something missing, something greater, deeper than the affection she had mistaken for love. It was hard to believe that the open-natured young man she had known was a criminal but the evidence was against him.

'You are very quiet, *querida*.' Carlos's caressing voice sent colour rushing into Jan's pale face. He was acting for his grandfather's benefit and reminding her that she wasn't pulling her weight. She forced a brilliant smile to her lips, her eyes shining silver, and Carlos caught his breath, while his grandfather glowered at her and started to talk, demanding his grandson's attention.

Alva and the *señora* seemed to find plenty to talk about and Jan, searching for something to say that wasn't either inane or irrelevant, heard Alva say. 'The divorce, it is easy in England, no?'

'No,' Jan said, though whether Alva was speaking to her or not she didn't know. 'There is no question of divorce between Carlos and me, if that is what you are hinting.' She looked directly at the girl and was pleased to see that for once she had pierced Alva's complacency.

'We only got married today,' Carlos said mildly. 'I have no intention of either divorcing Jacinta or of allowing her to divorce me or of talking about such unhappy things on my wedding day.' He thanked Mrs Kent who came in carrying a bottle of champagne and poured out the golden liquid and passed round the glasses.

'I will ask you to toast our marriage,' he said, standing up and pulling Jan with him.

The special dinner Mrs Kent had cooked could have been baked beans on toast for all the attention Jan paid it. She ate and drank, listening to but hearing very little of the desultory conversation. Alva also sat silent, her eyes fixed on Jan, their blankness pierced every now and then by a gleam that showed her brain was busy plotting something. Whatever it is, it isn't to my advantage, Jan said to herself, pushing her chocolate mousse round her plate and wishing the interminable meal would end.

'You do agree, don't you, Jacinta?' Carlos's impatient voice brought her head up to meet four pairs of dark eyes fixed on her.

'Agree to what, Carlos? I am afraid I didn't hear you.'

'Too busy thinking of her wedding night,' Alva said with a coarse little laugh that shocked Jan and caused her godmother's lips to firm to a thin line. Manuel del Raimondes looked at her as if he had never seen her before, Carlos frowned and looked disgusted, and Jan could have been sorry for the other girl as she saw the colour flood into her face if she hadn't at the same time been the recipient of a malevolent shaft from Alva's dark eyes.

'Grandfather would like to stay with us until next Friday then he, mother and Alva will go to London for a few days before going back to Spain. I have said we are willing to postpone our honeymoon until they leave. I can use the time to get things in order at the pottery before taking time off, if that suits you?' He held Jan's eyes with his. She murmured an assent and saw him relax.

'Where are you going for your honeymoon?' his grandfather asked. Carlos laughed and said it was a secret and the rest of the meal passed in discussing suitable resorts around the world. Listening to them, Jan was aware once again of how very wealthy Carlos was as he discussed the merits of South Sea Islands, China and Japan against the delights of a world tour in his private yacht, and yet again she wondered how she could have thought she could cope with such a lifestyle and, more important, how Carlos had ever thought she could fit in with him and his family.

She drifted into a daydream where she and Carlos loved each other and the honeymoon was a real one, not just a sham to deceive his grandfather, knowing as she dreamed that it would never come true, and wondering how long she should wait until she could say goodnight and go to bed. She saw Carlos looking at her intently, a gleam in his eyes, and knew he had once more read her mind.

'Was Alva right, *querida*? Are you thinking of the night we shall spend together?' Carlos's breath moved the strands of hair by her ear and rested warmly on her face, making the skin tingle as if he had touched it. He sat gracefully on the arm of her chair and, sliding his arm round her shoulders, pulled her against him, chuckling as she instinctively relaxed against him. 'It won't be long now, my Jacinta. Excuse yourself in thirty minutes; I will follow you very quickly.' It was an order, not a request. Jan glared at him resentfully, tilting her head back to meet his relentless expression. He would sound like a lover if anyone had overheard him but she knew that, though he wanted her, love was the last thing he would give.

He dropped a kiss on her upturned face and moved away as Alva held up her empty glass, smiling at him as if she were his bride and not Jan.

'So you have gained a prize not many women like you can hope for.' Señor del Raimondes's heavy accent kept Jan pinned in her chair. He seated himself on the end of the settee and, leaning forward, looked at her out of eyes so like his grandson's that Jan shivered. 'You do not answer me,' he said.

'I didn't think there was anything to answer,' Jan said spiritedly. 'You made a statement that merits no reply.'

His heavy brows drew together; he obviously wasn't used to young women who answered back.

'This marriage won't do,' he said, his accent thickening so much she had to strain to understand him. 'How much of my money will it take for you to leave this house tonight and never see my grandson again?' He leaned nearer to her. 'Come *señorita*, you can name your own price.'

Jan's mind registered the insulting offer and the equally insulting '*señorita*' as she shot from her chair. She drew herself up to her full height and in a low voice said, 'You insult both me and your grandson, *señor*.' Then turning on her heel, she walked out, her head high, though how she made it to her room without bursting into tears of rage and humiliation she never knew.

Safely inside the familiar room, Jan sank down on to her bed in a confusion of hatred of the old man and everyone else. No, not everyone. She wiped her tears from her eyes with her fingers as she had done as a child and confessed that no matter what Carlos had done, she loved him with every part of her, mind, body and soul. She was his completely and if she never saw him again he would always possess her and she would never be able to love any other man. She stared at the apricot carpet and shivered; the future looked black and empty.

Jan pushed her hand through her hair, lifting it away from her hot face and neck. What was it Carlos had said about her hair? Oh, yes, she remembered. He had compared it to a moonbeam; very poetical; that was his Spanish blood coming to the fore but it meant nothing, it was the kind of thing he would say to any girl. She stood up and untied the bows on her shoulders that held her dress in place. She had been so pleased with the pale peach silk. Cut very simply, it clung closely to her full breasts and outlined her slender waist and hips. The only ornaments were the bows edged with silver, but Carlos had only given her and it a cursory glance as she had entered the dining-room. Jan hadn't blamed him. Alva, in vivid scarlet outrageously tight, had had her arm twined in his and was smiling up at him in a way that left no doubt of how little she regarded Carlos's marriage.

Jan let her dress fall to the floor, stepping out of it as the door to Carlos's room opened. She held the soft silk defensively to her as he came swiftly across the room. He pulled the dress from her hands and tossed it on to a chair.

'Your dress is delightful, Jacinta, but without it you fill my senses and make me forget the way you rushed from the room without the courtesy of saying goodnight to our guests.' Jan flushed with embarrassment at Carlos's reproof of her bad manners and with anger as his grandfather's words came back to her.

'You should ask your grandfather what he said to me,' she snapped, disregarding the angry twist of Carlos's lips as she said his grandfather's name with all the contempt of which she was capable.

'My grandfather only welcomed you to our family. What was there in that to make you treat him as if he were a servant and not the head of our house?'

'I wouldn't treat any servant as I would like to treat that old man. All the servants I have known have been honest.'

'Are you implying my grandfather is not?' Carlos thundered. He gripped her arms and shook her, but Jan refused to falter though his rage sank knives into her heart.

'If your grandfather said he welcomed me into your family he was lying in his teeth. He offered me money, as much as I wanted, to leave here tonight and never see you again.' Carlos threw her from him so violently she fell against the side of the bed. He loomed over her and even in the pain she felt at his harsh treatment he had never looked so magnificent.

A *conquistador* and an eagle rolled into one. She felt laughter well up in her throat fighting with tears and knew that if she cried or laughed she wouldn't be able to stop. He hauled her to her feet and thrust her down on to the bed.

'It is you who are lying. My grandfather has no motive for offering you money. Even if you did leave here tonight you would still be my wife.'

'As Alva pointed out, there is such a thing as divorce, or annulment.'

'There will be neither. You are my wife and that is what you are going to remain. I shall make that quite clear to my family in the morning. As for you, my

Jacinta, after tonight you will not have any doubts.'

He followed her on to the bed, tossing aside the dark brown robe that was his only garment, and before Jan could protest he had unfastened her lacy bra and tossed it and her panties on to the floor.

'You are so very lovely, my Jacinta,' he said, burying his face in the valley between her breasts. His fingers teased her nipples to hardness as his mouth caressed hers with an expert sensuousness that dispersed all her defences like mist before the rising sun.

She moaned, opening her mouth to his invading tongue, and wound her arms round his neck, thrusting her fingers through his hair, delighting in the touch of silken crispness before running her hands across his shoulders and down his spine. She felt the muscles ripple under his smooth skin and gloried in the reactions she was causing.

'I want you to say you want me, Jacinta,' Carlos demanded and Jan gasped.

'You know I do.'

'Say it Jacinta,' he said huskily. 'I want to hear you.'

'I want you Carlos, but wanting isn't love.'

'It is more than enough, as you shall learn,' and his mouth closed over hers.

Jan arched against him, her hands and body telling him she was impatient for more than kisses. Carlos chuckled softly.

'Easy, my Jacinta. I want to savour every inch of you and we have all the time in the world.' The sharp ring of the telephone contradicted him and Jan tensed.

'We will not answer it; someone else can deal with it,' Carlos said and Jan melted against him as he stroked the soft skin of her inner thigh. The telephone stopped ringing and Carlos gently parted her thighs and closed his hand over the centre of her desire, only to swear and sit upright as someone pounded on the door.

He snatched a sheet to cover them as his grandfather threw the door open.

'I must remember to lock the door,' Carlos said furiously. 'To what do I owe this intrusion? Are you intending to throw Jacinta out of my house yourself, Grandfather?' The old man flinched and Jan was glad that Carlos appeared to believe her after all.

'There is a fire at the pottery. I am sorry to disturb you but it is important,' his grandfather said. Carlos sprang from the bed and started to dress.

'Are you also sorry for what you said to Jacinta this evening?' he asked, pulling on his trousers and reaching for his shirt. His grandfather's eyes travelled from his grandson to the girl, whose tumbled hair spread like molten silver over the sheet she clutched.

'If she is what you desire, then I accept her.' He nodded his imperious head and Jan thought he looked as much like an eagle as Carlos did. He would make a fine portrait, she mused, perhaps both men together: the young eagle and the old one.

'Jacinta.' Her attention came back to Carlos and she realised he had asked her something she hadn't heard. She focused her violet eyes on him and saw his own eyes darken with desire before his lashes concealed them.

'What did you say, Carlos? I am sorry, I didn't hear you.'

'There is trouble at the pottery; I will have to go. My mother and Alva are upset and as my wife you must stand in my stead while I am away.'

'I want to come with you,' Jan said, 'if you will give me a moment to get dressed . . .' Her voice trailed off at the impatience in both men's eyes.

'Grandfather will come with me; there is nothing you can do. Your place is here.' He thrust his grandfather out of the room and followed him, speaking over his shoulder. 'Do as I ask, *querida*. I shall be back as soon as I can.' The closing of the door prevented Jan from answering. She climbed out of bed and dressed in jeans and a pale green top, taking the first things that came to hand. She paused, her hand on her belt. Had his grandfather dreamed up the fire to prevent Carlos from making the marriage reality? She shook her head in self-disgust; there had been a telephone call and what would it benefit him? Their lovemaking had only been postponed, if the promise in Carlos's eyes was anything to go by.

She wasn't sure if she was sorry or relieved by the interruption. If it hadn't happened, she would have been committed even more deeply to Carlos than before and the parting, when it came, would be so much more painful. She sighed and pulled her hair back from her face, tying it with a black ribbon. However often they made love, or if they never did again, Carlos was part of her, in a way that bound her to him for all time.

She walked downstairs towards the sound of voices. The *señora* and Alva sounded more than disturbed.

'It is the fault of this horrible country,' the *señora* said, attacking Jan as she entered the room.

'What is?' Jan asked calmly, noting with interest that Alva's hair wasn't as thick or as long as it appeared when it was wound round her head and that Carlos's mother wore a thin satin robe in which she shivered.

'I will get you some coffee, *señora*,' Jan said. 'You look cold.'

'It is already ordered. Mrs Kent brings it.' Alva turned her back on Jan and stared into the fireplace.

'I think we should close the Derby pottery. There has been nothing but the upset,' said the *señora*, sitting down and pulling her robe closely round her.

Jan suppressed the anger she felt at the *señora's* talk of throwing men out of work and took the coffee tray from Mrs Kent.

'Thank you, you can go back to bed,' she said, smiling at the plump little woman.

'No, not yet. Perhaps we will wish something else,' the *señora* said sharply.

Mrs Kent looked at Jan enquiringly.

'It's all right, Mrs Kent. If there is anything more needed, I will see to it.'

'Thank you, Mrs del Raimondes.' And Mrs Kent left the room, pointedly ignoring the Spanish woman who glared after her in the manner of an angry cat deprived of its fish.

'How dare you countermand my orders to the servants? My son shall hear of this.'

'I dare because I am Carlos's wife, I am mistress here and Mrs Kent works for me.'

The *señora* banged her cup down on to the tray, rose and, with an aplomb worthy of a prima donna, walked out of the room. Jan wanted to clap but thought better of it as an angry Alva stormed after her, turning in the doorway to add,

'Carlos will not be pleased how you treat his mother. In Spain we are taught to be polite to older persons.'

Another good exit, and she could be right; Carlos wouldn't like her putting his mother in her place. Jan sipped her coffee thoughtfully. She had a nasty feeling that despite what he had said he would be angry, especially if Alva got in with her version first. She finished her coffee and decided to go to bed. Carlos had said she was to take charge and she had tried to do just that, but look how it had turned out.

Moonlight filled the hall and on impulse Jan opened the door and ran down the steps. She strolled round the house and down the path leading to a small lake, round which she had promised herself she would plant shrubs, small trees and spring flowers. She had lots of plans for the garden but now she wondered if she would be here long enough to carry any of them out. Carlos seemed determined to make their marriage work but once his grandfather was resigned to it how long would his resolution last? She leaned against the trunk of a silver birch and looked at the peaceful water and wished she felt as calm, but her love for Carlos was a torment and a delight and she didn't know which was the uppermost.

CHAPTER ELEVEN

THERE was a soft rustle and Jan looked up to see a man standing in front of her.

'Carlos?' she said tentatively, knowing as she spoke that it wasn't him.

'Surely you haven't forgotten me, Jan?' He reached out a hand and touched her cheek, moving so the moonlight shone on his face.

'Wade?' she breathed, hardly able to believe her eyes.

'In the flesh.' He laughed softly and Jan caught her breath. So many times had she wished Wade was standing before her, so often had she dreamed she heard him laugh in just that way, only to find it had just been her imagination, and now he was here and she didn't know what to say.

He came closer and bent his head to kiss her, but Jan moved and put a hand on his arm, warding him off.

'What's the matter, Jan? Don't you want my kisses now you're living in the big man's house?' There was a sneer in his tone that Jan didn't like.

'You didn't answer my letter, Wade, or come when I needed you. Why are you here now? What do you want?'

'What would you say if I said I want you? I should have answered your letter but there were reasons why I didn't. It was bad enough that you were suspected; what good would it have done if it was known you and I were in love?'

'Were we in love, Wade? I don't think you were or

169

you would have come to me, even if you had been suspected—and there was no reason you should have been, was there? You could have cleared my name, Wade, and when I phoned you, you said you had done just that, but you weren't very convincing and I don't think you tried very hard.' She was struck by his stillness and in that moment many things became clear.

'It was you, Wade. You stole the formula and left me to take the blame. I am right, aren't I?'

'Oh, come on, Jan, don't be like that. You weren't supposed to get caught.'

'No? Then why did you send me to the wrong offices if not to act as your scapegoat? You knew the theft would be found out and I was in the right place with a stupid excuse while you already had what you wanted.' Jan's eyes blazed scornfully. Wade moved uneasily, the clear, cold light making his features take on a shifty look Jan had never noticed before.

'I didn't mean it that way, Jan. I took the formula earlier that morning and I thought you would provide a useful red herring if I had been seen.'

'Carlos was convinced you were in Spain.'

Wade grinned. 'A bit of smart cover-up. I don't suppose he bothered to mention I had to ring him back, which I did, from England. I'm sorry you've had a rough time; I'll make it up to you. That wasn't the right formula, as I am sure you know, but with your help I won't fail again.'

'With my help?' Jan said faintly.

'You're in a unique position now, Jan, actually living in his house. I couldn't believe you had been so clever when David told me.'

'David?' Jan said vaguely. This couldn't be true. Wade couldn't be in so deep. Even though she knew she didn't love him, had never loved him as she loved Carlos, she had held on to the thought that it had all been a horrible mistake and that against all odds the formula would prove to have been mislaid. But now Wade had admitted to the theft.

'You met him in the park, remember?' said Wade impatiently. Jan snapped out of her daze and pushed herself away from the tree.

'Of course I remember. He's the boss of this whole thing, isn't he?'

'Bright girl. Dave's the brains behind it, but he isn't the boss. We're partners and he hates Carlos del Raimondes as much as I do.'

'Why should you hate him? He's done nothing to you.' Jan said, a slight quiver in her voice. Even to think of someone hating Carlos sent fear running through her veins.

'I hate all rich bastards. Why should he have all this while I have to slave for every penny?' Wade waved his arms to encompass the house and grounds, a look on his face that made Jan slump back against the tree again, feeling she was going to faint. Wade really did hate Carlos and her every instinct told her he was dangerous.

'Carlos works hard,' she protested.

'I bet he does. Well, we intend he shall share some of the fruits of his hard work.' He turned to Jan and reached out for her. 'That's where you come in, Jan. I don't know what the hell you're doing here, but you can help us.'

'No, Wade, I won't help you do anything.' She side-stepped and the moonlight caught her ring, making it blaze.

'What's that?' Wade grasped her hand in his and

looked at the huge emerald and the heavy wedding ring unbelievingly.

'I am married to Carlos, so you must leave me out of your plans.' She turned to go, but Wade gripped her hand harder.

'Oh no you don't, Jan. You will help me, even if you have gone over to the enemy. I think I'm glad you married him; you won't want any harm to come to the bastard, will you?'

Jan felt icy cold waves ripple through her. She let the hand she had lifted to hit Wade with drop to her side. He laughed mockingly and she wondered how she could ever have thought him attractive.

'I think you had better go, Wade. Carlos could come looking for me at any moment,' she said, wishing hard that her longing for him would bring him to her. Wade laughed again, the note of exaltation chilling her afresh.

'He has his hands too full to come looking for a straying wife.'

'What do you mean by that?' Jan said, meaning to run the moment she got her hand free.

'We arranged a small diversion. When I knew you were here I had to speak to you and I couldn't get near you any other way.'

'You set the fire in the pottery?'

'Not me. Dave. And next time it won't be a harmless fire in an outbuilding; it could be a bomb—and not only here; we have contacts in Spain.'

Jan stared at him in horror.

'Hey, that's a great idea! To set bombs to go off in both factories at the same time. I must suggest it to Dave.'

'Why are you doing this, Wade?' Jan asked quietly. There was something in Wade's manner that frightened her more than the threats, terrible though they were. He seemed on the brink of madness. He was standing with his head thrown back, his hair touched to a burnished gold by the moon. So must the knights of old have looked as they pledged their lives to their kings, but the king Wade served was self-interest and, unlike the knights, he had thrown honour away.

'I want that formula, Jan. I have a customer for it.'

She shook her head in bewilderment.

'Your uncle left you a great deal of money. Why should you want more?' She stiffened as Wade smiled, the old warm-hearted smile, and for a moment time rolled back and the Wade she had loved looked out of the eyes of the stranger he had become.

'You didn't really believe in my uncle, did you, Jan? Oh, lord, you really were an innocent. I made that up to get back to this country.'

'To steal the formula for the glaze, and you found me ready to hand?'

'As you are now.'

'I won't do it, Wade. I shall tell Carlos.'

'Will he believe you, and can you risk harm coming to him? If you don't help me, Jan, you will never know when those bombs will go off, or where. The police can't protect him for the rest of his life.'

Jan stared into Wade's cold eyes and shuddered inwardly. The young man she had known had changed into a monster. She didn't realise she had spoken her thoughts aloud until Wade's eyes narrowed.

'Call me all the names you can think of, Jan, but you will do as I want.'

'And that is?' Jan threw her head back defiantly, but she knew she would have to do as he said.

'Get me that formula. I don't care how you do it or

how difficult it is but get it. You have two days. I will be here on Sunday night, same time.' He released her hand and slipped into the shadows before she could speak.

The path to the house seemed a mile long. Jan stumbled into the hall and upstairs and into her room, dreading that Carlos's mother or Alva would appear and demand to know where she had been, but the house was silent. She closed her door feeling she had reached sanctuary after a dangerous journey. She undressed, showered and got into bed, trying to hold her thoughts at bay, but as soon as she lay down they came back in full force.

There was no doubt in her mind that Wade had meant exactly what he said. He would find some way of harming Carlos if she didn't get what he wanted. Terror-stricken ideas flowed through her brain. Pictures of Carlos injured or, even worse, lying in the midst of the devastation caused by a bomb, were so vivid she shook with fear. She couldn't risk any harm coming to him, she must do what Wade had ordered her to do. There was no way she could go to the offices and if she did she wouldn't know where to start looking. She sat up with a jerk.

Carlos had said he wanted to clear his workload so they could have a honeymoon. It was possible he would bring documents home, but would the formula be one of them? She lay down again. She was so tired, she couldn't think any more. She could only hope she would have a chance to do what she had to do. No glaze, no matter how unique, was worth risking Carlos's life for.

Jan woke the next morning with a feeling of dread. As soon as she opened her eyes she remembered the meeting with Wade and his threats against Carlos—and not only Carlos. There would be, must be, others involved in any explosions. She felt sick at the very thought of the carnage set off by greed. She turned her head slowly, half hoping, half fearing to see Carlos, but the other side of the bed was empty, the bedclothes unrumpled, the pillow smooth. She showered and dressed in a sleeveless pink cotton dress, picked up the matching short-sleeved jacket and went downstairs, telling herself that he had been so late after dealing with the fire that he had hesitated to disturb her. Desperately trying to believe her own explanation, she walked into the drawing-room to see Carlos and Alva standing very close together with every appearance of having been exchanging confidences for a long time.

At Jan's appearance their low-voiced conversation came to a halt and Alva, with a gloating look, brushed past Jan and walked out of the room, her footsteps beating out a triumphant rhythm. Jan forgot Alva as she walked across the room to Carlos. He was casually dressed in designer jeans and a deep cream silk sweater and she thought he looked even more virile and masculine than he did in his more formal clothes.

'Good morning, Carlos,' she said, smiling warmly and wondering if he would kiss her. After all, they were married, even if it wasn't a normal marriage and their wedding night was still to come. Carlos stood quite still, only his eyes betraying he had heard her.

'What is good about this morning?' he said at last. 'If you think I am going to play the loving bridegroom you are mistaken. I have to go to the office so you must amuse yourself.'

Jan drew an angry breath. 'I don't want you to play any kind of bridegroom,' she said furiously. 'I was just being polite. You told us last night you had work to do before we could go on our farce of a honeymoon.'

'So I did,' he said softly, his eyes as cold as the winter in Jan's heart. 'I have decided to bring my papers home and work on them this weekend. That way I can also keep important documents safe.'

'By important documents I suppose you mean the correct formula of your new glaze?'

'Among others, yes. Does the glaze have a special interest for you?'

Jan turned away to pour out a cup of tea. For one dreadful moment it seemed as if he suspected something. She took a tight hold on her nerves; it was just her guilty conscience. She forced a smile and buttered a piece of toast, the rasp of the knife against the bread almost more than she could stand.

'I am only interested because you have accused me of trying to steal it,' she said, lifting a square of toast to her lips.

'It is strange that you have done nothing to convince me of your innocence. You still maintain my belief is false.'

'Of course it is, and there is nothing else I can do to convince you,' Jan flashed, then checked as the realisation hit her that if she carried out Wade's orders she would be as guilty as Carlos thought her.

'Does your grandfather know about the theft?' she faltered.

'No, and he is not to know. All hope of him accepting you would be lost if he thought my wife stole for gain.' His eyes narrowed and Jan could have wept at the suspicion that flared in them.

'Then why should he offer me as much money as I want to get out of your life?'

'My grandfather is as wary of women as I am, but he made an error there. As my wife you will gain far more than he can give you, so don't try to make me think you are noble. No woman is when it comes to money.' He turned on his heel and Jan swallowed the toast with an effort, watching Carlos as, after a perfunctory 'see you later', he strode from the room.

She hadn't thought of what would happen if she succeeded in delivering the papers to Wade and now the hopelessness of her situation overwhelmed her. She wouldn't be able to hide what she had done, and worst of all Carlos would think she had been involved with Wade from the beginning. But what else could she do? She had to stop Wade from planting bombs at any cost to herself.

Should she tell Carlos the whole thing and let him set a trap for Wade? If she did, and Wade escaped, Carlos would still be in danger. There were so many ways a man could die and Wade was determined Carlos should pay in one way or the other. No, she couldn't take the risk; she had to steal the glaze somehow.

It was surprisingly easy. Carlos had been careless, leaving his study unlocked while strolling with Alva in the garden on the Sunday afternoon. Jan had excused herself and made towards her room, trying the study door as a last desperate resort. Carlos hadn't left the room all day Saturday or Sunday morning, even taking his lunch at his desk, and apart from dinner they hadn't seen him until he had joined them for tea an hour earlier. His manner to Jan had remained cold and remote, as if she didn't exist on the same planet, while he had warmed to Alva, much to her delight.

Jan sighed and turned the handle of the study door again. Had it yielded? Yes, the door wasn't locked. She darted into the room, hardly able to believe her luck. On the desk was a pile of papers and Jan's heart sank. It would take hours to go through them. She lifted the top one and underneath saw the familiar blue formula. She grasped it quickly, tucked it into the waistband of the green skirt she was wearing and pulled the matching silk jumper over it.

Holding her breath, she raced upstairs and into her room, locking the door behind her. She examined her prize, fearful that it wasn't the genuine one, but it appeared to be the right one and Jan pushed it under a pile of tights until she could give it to Wade.

The next few hours crawled by. Now she was committed, Jan wanted to get it over with. Only when Wade had the formula in his hands would she feel Carlos was safe. At last the hands of the clock told her it was time to meet Wade and she excused herself from the drawing-room, where Betty had just brought in the coffee, feeling as if she were walking to the gallows.

'I have a bad headache. I am sure, *señora*, you will be kind enough to pour the coffee for me. I must lie down.'

'Are you sure, Jacinta? Wouldn't you rather walk in the garden with me?' Carlos's question was further torture to Jan's overstretched nerves. There was nothing she would like more than to stroll in the moonlight with him. He had never asked her before and that he should do so now was more than she could stand. She shook her head and left the room before the tears could steal down her face. As quietly as she could, she retrieved the document and made her way out of the house.

The garden stretched before her, a place of night-mares and shadows; the moon, so lovely when she had strolled under its rays two nights before, was now a cold menace, lighting her treachery. She reached the birch tree and leaned against it, as exhausted as if she had run from Derby. She jumped at a stir in the bushes, forcing herself to relax as nothing happened. Carlos's face swam before her eyes but before she could dwell on the mental picture it was replaced by Alva's image, her eyes lit with malice.

When her marriage to Carlos was over, as it must be after tonight, would he please his grandfather and make Alva his bride? Her heart sank as she thought of the Spanish girl sharing his life as she, Jan, longed to do. Alva wouldn't give Carlos the love he needed if he was to ever recover from the bitterness Alison had fostered. If she had thought he would be happy with Alva, she would step down and try to be thankful. Jan ran her fingers over the smooth bark of the tree and sighed. She would have no chance of remaining once Carlos found out what she had done.

She was so engrossed in her thoughts, she didn't hear Wade until he touched her.

'Jan,' he said, satisfaction oozing from him. 'Have you got it?' He held out his hand and Jan looked from it to his face. Perhaps it was the moonlight, but Wade could have sat for a painting of greed as he looked at that moment.

'How can anyone take the risk of using it, Wade? Carlos will know at once that it is his.'

'He may know,' Wade jeered, 'but proving it is another matter. Come on, Jan, don't be so stupid. It's done all the time. Now give me the papers before someone else comes out for a moonlight walk.' He reached for the document but Jan held it tightly, shaking her head.

'I want your assurance that you won't harm Carlos if I give it to you.'

'You do, do you? Fallen in love with him, have you, Jan? It won't do you any good even if you are married.

As soon as it serves his purpose he will divorce you.'

'I know that,' Jan said, the pain Wade's words caused making it difficult to speak.

'Yet you still want to keep him safe?'

'As you said, Wade, I love Carlos. I would give my life for him and his not loving me can't alter that. I want your promise, or I shall scream and you won't get away.'

'I promise. I won't do anything to your precious Carlos or his pottery.' His voice softened, bringing back memories of a Wade she had known in what seemed another life. 'Come with me, Jan. You have no future here. Once del Raimondes finds out, you will land in jail. We could make a great team.'

'No, thank you, Wade. I will take my chance with Carlos.'

'Even if it means prison and divorce?'

'Even so,' Jan said steadily. Wade looked at her with regret and held out his hand. Jan quietly gave him the paper but the moment he grasped it, it was whipped from him.

'I will take that,' Carlos said, his other hand falling heavily on Wade's shoulder. The open space under the tree filled with uniformed men and Jan crouched against the tree, her eyes wide, as Wade was arrested, cautioned and taken away.

Her eyes fixed on Carlos, Jan felt her worst dreams had come true. She braced herself for the contempt she was sure she would receive and was astounded when he scooped her up into his arms.

'Carlos,' she faltered. 'What are you doing?'

'Taking you home,' he murmured softly and Jan quivered as his voice wrapped round her, almost like a caress. She gave up trying to understand and nestled against him, putting her arms round his neck and letting her head fall on to his shoulder. Just for these few minutes she would pretend that Carlos loved her, even if it meant the awakening would be all the harder for her dream.

They entered the house and Jan thought they would get to their rooms without anyone seeing them, but as Carlos put his foot on the first stair his grandfather ran down, looking like an eagle about to pounce.

'What are you doing with Jacinta?' he roared, waving a paper that she recognised as one of her drawings. Carlos raised his eyebrows.

'I am taking her to bed. She is my wife,' he said mildly. His grandfather looked at him enquiringly and Carlos grinned. 'Everything is taken care of,' he said. Jan looked from one to the other, but before she could say anything the old man waved the drawing again and she saw it was the one of Carlos and the eagle.

'She is also the daughter of an old friend,' his grandfather said in a muted roar.

'So?' Carlos began.

'How did you know?' Jan asked.

'You signed this.' Grandfather tapped the drawing with a gnarled finger. 'You have the same initials as your father and a lot of the same style.'

'I'm not as good,' Jan said, stating a fact she had come to terms with long ago.

'Nonsense, girl, you are very good. This portrait shows a lot of talent.'

Carlos put Jan gently on her feet and, keeping an arm round her, reached for the drawing. His grandfather let it go reluctantly and Carlos studied it for, to Jan, long tense minutes. He gave the drawing back to his grandfather and tightened his arm round Jan.

'You have been holding out on me. Your design work

is excellent but this is something else altogether. We will discuss it tomorrow—yes, Grandfather, with you—but now ...' he swung Jan back into his arms and strode upstairs '. . . we have something more important to talk about.'

And to his grandfather's gruff, 'Treat her gently, boy, she has gone through a lot these last few days,' he gave a quiet rejoinder in Spanish that made the old man chuckle.

Carlos walked rapidly to his bedroom, kicked the door shut behind him and laid Jan carefully on the bed and sat on the edge facing her.

'I agree with grandfather,' he said.

'What about?' Jan put a hand to her head. Too much had happened too fast. She had expected Carlos to display the deadly anger that paralysed her. Instead he was acting like a lover, and Grandfather, of all people, so eager to get her out of Carlos's life he was willing to hand over a fortune, was coming to her defence in no uncertain manner.

'Are you all right, Jacinta? Have you got a headache? Should I send for a doctor?' Carlos sounded so anxious that Jan put her hand on his, to have it grasped so tightly she gasped.

'Oh, Jacinta, I have hurt you, and that is the last thing I want to do.' He pressed his lips to her palm and she gasped again as her nerves tingled at his touch.

'I'm all right, Carlos. As your grandfather said, it has been a trying time.' She looked at him beseechingly. 'I know it looks black, Carlos, and I did steal the papers this time but ...' Her words were halted by Carlos placing his hand gently over her lips.

'Don't, *querida*,' he said harshly. 'Don't remind me of all the dreadful things I accused you of. I know now that they weren't true.' He stroked her hair as it spread over the pillow. 'I don't think I really believed them, even as I hurled them at you.'

Jan sat up, holding on to his arm, conscious of the muscles under his jacket.

'You could have me sent to prison for what I did today,' she said gravely.

'I have every intention of doing just that,' Carlos said, equally solemnly. He gathered her into his arms as alarm flared in her eyes. 'I shall never let you out of the prison of our marriage, my Jacinta. My arms will form the bars and my kisses your punishment.' Jan gave herself up to the love she saw in his eyes and, raising her face to his, was swept away into a heaven she had only dreamed of as his mouth covered hers.

He undressed her slowly, kissing every inch he uncovered, and Jan felt deprived when he stood up to remove his own clothes. She welcomed him back, winding her arms round him. She pressed against him, arching her back in a frenzy to join with him in the age-old way. Carlos cupped her breast with one hand, bent his dark head and closed his lips gently over her nipple. Jan shuddered, pleasure, so intense it bordered on pain, coursing through her body. She moaned softly and felt Carlos react to the sound. He parted her thighs gently and took the possession she gladly granted him.

An ocean roared, crashing against impassable cliffs. Jan rode on the crest of a wave again and again until at last she drifted into quiet waters. She opened her eyes dreamily. This was what she was on earth for and here was where she belonged. Carlos's arms tightened round her.

'I love you, my Jacinta,' he said huskily and Jan closed her eyes, every muscle in her body tensing then relaxing as she realised she was dreaming. But Carlos's kiss wasn't a dream, nor was the anxious look in his eyes, nor the worried note in his voice.

'Are you all right? I wasn't too rough, was I?' He groaned. 'Of course I was, and now you are disgusted with me.' Jan trailed her fingers down his face to his lips.

'You weren't too rough. I liked it.'

'Then what is it? You tensed against me. I felt your rejection in every part of me.'

'I didn't reject you. It was reaction from what you said, or rather what I thought you said.'

'What was that, my Jacinta?' he asked, laughter just below the surface.

Jan blushed and he kissed the fingers hovering near his mouth.

'If you thought I said I love you, you were quite right. I do and if you don't tell me you love me I think I shall die.' The serious note had Jan's arms flying round him.

'I do love you, Carlos. I have for a long time but I thought you hated me and I didn't blame you. How could you love anyone as dreadful as I seemed to be?'

'I asked myself that many times, especially when I thought you had conspired to steal from me, but it was already too late. You were the spirit of loveliness, the very essence of womanhood, the woman I had searched for in my dreams and never hoped to find, and when I did you had my wallet in your hands counting the money. I wanted to kill you for destroying an ideal I hadn't known I cherished.'

Jan murmured a protest and Carlos trailed kisses across her mouth. 'I think I knew even then that you were looking for an address, but I refused to admit that any woman could be honest. I spent the next few days trying to get you out of my mind but you were with me every moment and when you walked into my office and said you were Jacinta Shelley, the woman I thought had stolen from my firm, anger black as hell overwhelmed me. I will never know how I kept my hands off you. I didn't know whether I wanted to strangle you or take you there and then on the office floor. Only disgust that I should even want to touch the woman I thought you were saved you.

'From then on I fought a losing battle and during the days of your suspension from the pottery I racked my brains for a way to keep you with me.' He smiled wickedly. 'As you know, I found one.'

Jan rubbed her cheek against his, loving the masculine scent of warm skin and something that was only Carlos.

'I don't understand what happened tonight. How did you know I was meeting Wade in the garden?'

Carlos captured her hand and stroked it, making her shiver in anticipation.

'I have known about Felton for some time. The only thing that wasn't clear was how far your involvement with him went. For a long time I thought he was your lover, until proved otherwise.' He chuckled as she squirmed against him at the memory of how he had gained his knowledge. 'I wanted to tell you I suspected he and David Long were behind the theft, but you were engaged to him and I thought you loved him.'

'I know now it wasn't love, not as I love you,' she murmured.

'Are you sure you do love me? I made you work so hard.'

'I hated you for that,' Jan said, gasping as his arms tightened round her. 'But tonight, how did you know about that?' she asked again, burying her face against him. He lifted her head gently until she met his eyes.

'Alva saw you meet Felton on Friday,' he said gently. 'I knew he was in the district and I thought he might try to contact you, so she did us both a good turn, though that wasn't her intention.' He kissed her, his lips lingering on hers, and Jan snuggled closer to him.

'I hated having to take the formula from your study.' She glared at him indignantly. 'You knew all along that I would look on your desk. It was a trap.'

Carlos touched her cheek, stroking the soft skin. 'I hated putting you through that, my Jacinta, but it was necessary. We had to catch Felton with the document in his possession.'

Jan struggled to sit upright. 'Carlos, Wade has a partner ready to set bombs at the pottery here and in Spain,' she said urgently.

He drew her gently down, cradling her in his arms. 'Hush, *querida*, we have David Long safe.'

Jan relaxed against him. 'Then that's all right.' She ran a finger round his lips. 'Are you sure you don't still love Alison, Carlos.'

'I am very sure, my Jacinta. I have not loved her for years. There have been other women, but I have loved none of them until you came along and turned my world upside down.'

'Do you really love me?'

'Do you need to ask that, my Jacinta?'

'Not really. I just like to hear you say it.' She looked at him enquiringly. 'You haven't asked me the same thing . . .' Her eyes widened and delicate colour stole into her face at the expression in his eyes. 'You heard what I said to Wade, didn't you? Oh, lord, did all those policemen hear me?'

'No, *querida*, the policemen weren't near enough to hear, but I heard you say you loved me and would die for me.' He buried his face in her hair. 'I, too, would die for you, Jacinta, but I would much prefer it if we both lived. You bargained for my safety even though you thought I would have you flung into prison, or at least cut you out of my life. Oh, *querida*, if you knew how humble I felt at that moment and how I thanked God for the chance to show you how much I adore you.' He rained kisses on her face and throat until Jan thought she would go up in flames.

'You will give me that chance?'

He sounded uncertain, his whole body tensing against her as he waited for her answer. Jan, looking into the future, saw sunshine and shadow, but whatever came their way wouldn't matter as long as they had each other. She drew him close to her and murmured exactly what he wanted to hear.

Harlequin Intrigue

Two exciting new stories each month.

Each title mixes a contemporary, sophisticated romance with the surprising twists and turns of a puzzler...romance with "something more."

Because romance can be quite an adventure.

Intrg-1

Romance, Suspense and Adventure

Harlequin Superromance

**Here are the longer, more involving stories you
have been waiting for . . . Superromance.**

Modern, believable novels of love, full of the complex
joys and heartaches of real people.

Intriguing conflicts based on today's constantly
changing life-styles.

Four new titles every month.
Available wherever paperbacks are sold.

SUPER-1

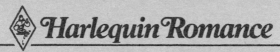 **Harlequin Romance**

Coming Next Month

2953 BLIND TO LOVE Rebecca Winters
When Libby Anson joins her husband in Kenya, she's shocked
by his announcement that their marriage is over. He insists that
his blindness changes everything. But it doesn't—not for Libby.

2954 FETTERS OF GOLD Jane Donnelly
Nic is in love with Dinah. Although Dinah isn't as sure of her
feelings for Nick, there's no way she'll let his overbearing
cousin Marcus dictate what they can or cannot do!

2955 UNEXPECTED INHERITANCE Margaret Mayo
Alice is far from delighted at the prospect of a visit to the
West Indies, all expenses paid. It means giving in to the
commands of her unknown grandfather's will. Worse still, it
means seeing Jared Duvall again....

2956 WHEN TWO PATHS MEET Betty Neels
Katherine is properly grateful to Dr. Jason Fitzroy for rescuing
her from the drudgery of her brother's household and helping
her to find a new life-style. She can't help dreaming about him,
though she's sure he's just being kind.

2957 THE CINDERELLA TRAP Kate Walker
Dynamic Matt Highland doesn't connect the stunning model
Clea with the plump unattractive teenager he'd snubbed years
ago. But Clea hasn't forgotten—or forgiven—and she devises a
plan to get even!

2958 DEVIL MOON Margaret Way
Career girl Sara is a survivor in the jungle of the television
world, but survival in the real jungle is a different matter, as she
finds out when her plane crashes. There, she is dependent on
masterful Guy Trenton to lead the party to safety....

Available in January wherever paperback books are sold, or
through Harlequin Reader Service:

In the U.S.
901 Fuhrmann Blvd.
P.O. Box 1397
Buffalo, N.Y. 14240-1397

In Canada
P.O. Box 603
Fort Erie, Ontario
L2A 5X3

Step into a world of pulsing adventure, gripping emotion and lush sensuality with these evocative love stories penned by today's best-selling authors in the highest romantic tradition. Pursuing their passionate dreams against a backdrop of the past's most colorful and dramatic moments, our vibrant heroines and dashing heroes will make history come alive for you.

Watch for two new Harlequin Historicals each month, available wherever Harlequin books are sold. History was never so much fun—you won't want to miss a single moment!